MYTRO

JOHN BIGGS

RAY BRIDGE PRESS

For Kasper

MYTRO

CHAPTER ONE

The Door in the Rock

Huffing and puffing, Turtle Fulton ran another few feet while the Kincaid twins, Nate and Nick, Nick, with his long, wavy blonde hair, and Nate, with his short blonde buzz, came up behind him, barely winded. They were running a practice race in Central Park, and as the slowest member of the school's already slow track team, Turtle expected the brothers to laugh as they roared past. Instead, they turned around to look at him and then veered off into some bushes. They waited there while Turtle ran at his own pace, slow and steady. His real name was Paul but his plodding gait gave him his nickname. He didn't mind it. Slow and steady won the race, after all.

Turtle ran a few more feet, counting his footsteps in his head as he ran, breathing out on every prime number between 2 and 11—2, 3, 5, 7, 11—a trick he used to keep himself distracted on the longer runs. His track coach said he was good at distances, and exercises like this made him better, but the Kincaids were always faster and always first.

Now, they were doing something weird.

As he stopped to glance back, he saw them turn and rummage through a cluster of tall green bushes topped by purple flowers growing on the face of a towering rock. They moved farther into the greenery, submerging themselves like they were hiding. Weird, yes, but Turtle kept running—until the rustling stopped.

Turtle halted midstride. From out of the bushes came something that sounded like a surge of wind , and when Turtle turned to look again, the twins were gone. They had vanished into the bushes.

Where did they go? What was that noise?

He ran over to the rock, a few feet off the path. He could feel his heart rate rising, his pulse booming in his ears. The scent of the flowers on the bushes was strong in the air, even over the sharp smell of fresh asphalt coming from somewhere nearby.

Scratching his shoulder through his Manhattan Friends Track Team T-shirt, Turtle tried to think. A jackhammer that had been thrumming through the air stopped, and the trill of birds replaced it in the quiet. Somewhere over a low hill, Turtle heard the sound of traffic—the whine of hydraulics as a bus stopped, a horn beeping once in warning, the rev of a high-powered motorcycle peeling out into the street. The rest of the team was somewhere far ahead, but there were more pressing matters.

Where could the Kincaids be?

Turtle parted the bushes, convinced the twins were hiding there, somewhere, but it took only a few seconds to confirm what he had suspected: the boys were gone.

The stone behind the bushes looked like the wall of a forgotten, ruined castle, the edges chiseled roughly at right angles and the cracks filled with brown dust. Someone had carved the number 13 into the rock, although the carving was old and worn down to near invisibility. It reminded him of the vague, permanent graffiti that Turtle had become used to seeing in the city, although this was a bit tamer than some of the stuff he had seen written on other Central Park rocks.

His grandmother had told him that all the huge rocks in Central Park had been quarried north of the city then brought in on horse-drawn wagons—what a wild thought. This rock alone was a monster. Bigger than a small house, it had been taken from the earth and placed here as a decoration.

As the jackhammer pounded again, drowning out the sound of Turtle's own heartbeat, he reached out to feel the cold rock and the grit of the mud that had sluiced off the top and dried on its surface. There was nowhere for the twins to have gone. Wiping his sweaty brow, Turtle faced a blank wall of stone, his hands searching for hidden handles or buttons.

Was this a magic trick? he thought.

Waffle-patterned footprints scuffed the dust at the base of the wall, and Turtle saw the faint imprint of a Nike swoosh in a patch of drying mud. He put his own foot next to the fresh track; it was about his size—and about Nick's and Nate's size too. So they had been here. He wasn't dreaming.

Turtle turned around. The grass leading up to where the twins disappeared was worn away, and the dirt showed through. The park had always been crisscrossed with little, informal walkways, but this was the first time Turtle had seen one end at a blank stone wall.

Turtle knew you weren't supposed to follow paths in Central Park for a couple reasons. First, you weren't allowed to walk on most of the grass, and second, it was supposedly dangerous. As he stared at the rock and the little path that led up to it, Turtle felt a sense of dread—and excitement.

In the distance, someone laid on a car horn, long and loud. Turtle ignored the circus of sound that surrounded him and wondered if the twins had climbed to the top and over.

Slowly, cautiously, he rubbed his hand along the surface of the stone again—feeling foolish. He was dead last in the practice race; the rest of the team was already far ahead.

Just as he was about to give up and resume running, Turtle felt a deep rumble under his feet. He placed a hand on the cold stone surface and listened. He felt it more than heard it, but there it was—

the rumble again, like a train roaring by. He put his ear against the rock wall and it was louder—*clack clack ... clack clack*—a subway train rattling on iron rails, a sound that was so impossible to miss that it gave him a chill.

There was a train behind the wall.

Engrossed, Turtle didn't notice that he was falling forward until the rock face gave way, moving inward on invisible hinges. Dust cascaded down on him as he started to fall, he held out his hands to break his descent, but there was nothing to stop him, just a rush of air.

He was inside the rock.

The door shut quickly behind him with a mighty whoosh.

He had popped through and onto a subway platform. On this side, the door he had fallen through was clad in heavy wood and held together with polished iron bands. The iron was beautifully wrought and the wood was covered in delicate carving, the planks polished to a bright golden sheen. Birds took wing from long grass carved in the rich, deep wood. Everything was carved in deep relief and with great care. Sharp letters along the top of the door read: "Central Park South."

Turtle tried to push his way back out, but the door wouldn't budge.

The *clack clack* was wildly loud here, and Turtle took a quick breath and crouched down, ready to run. But where? The door behind him was closed and the platform was only about fifty feet wide and ten feet deep.

Turtle stared, dumbstruck, at the twins, who just stood there like they were waiting for the train. They hadn't noticed him. Something was coming down the tunnel. The wind and dust picked up and filled the platform with noise.

Was it a New York subway platform? It wasn't dirty or crowded or full of noise and mess. It was delicately gas-lit from above with crystal chandeliers. It smelled sweet and close, like a church; the scent of the polish and pine almost made Turtle sleepy. There was also a whiff of smoke from somewhere and the smell of ozone, like the water from a garden hose. The walls were inlaid with pieces of polished brass and tile the color of a robin's egg, coated with crackled glaze. The ceiling swung up above them, into the darkness. Tracks led forward and backward into dark tunnels. Turtle could feel his heart beating in his ears and heard his own labored breathing—as well as the twins' laughter.

Next to the door was a wooden booth with glass windows. A tombstone-shaped opening was cut into the lower part of the glass, and a ticket machine made of wrought iron poked out of the counter, a length of connected tickets sticking out of the window like a tongue. A carefully hand-lettered sign, yellowed with age, read: "Closed Until Further Notice."

Nick and Nate were standing on the platform as a train rolled into the station with a wild screech. "What the ...," whispered Turtle, and Nick suddenly turned around, his eyes wide with surprise. Nate followed, and then they looked at each other.

"What are you doing here?" asked Nick.

"Who let you in?" asked Nate.

"I saw you go into the bushes and I fell through and I saw you guys ...," said Turtle.

Nate and Nick looked at each other again, angrily, then at Turtle. Nick scowled.

"Didn't you lock it after, Nate? How the heck did he get in?"

"There is no lock," said Nate. "It just closes."

The station filled with sound and light as a train streaked out of the south end of the tunnel and stopped abruptly, its brakes squealing.

It wasn't a modern train. It had a gas headlight and consisted of two long cars coupled together. They were painted a deep crimson that was almost brown and had black iron front and back platforms. Two red lights blinked on the burnished copper roof, and the front and back of each sloped gently down, making the train look almost like a centipede. The wheels rattled against the rails as it stopped, and the cars heaved forward before settling on their springs as the doors—two on each car—swung back and in, hissing compressed air as they did. The train sat idling on the tracks.

Despite their outdated style, the train cars looked brand new, washed and polished to a shine. They had been carefully maintained and, unlike normal subway trains, the steel wheels were still glossy and bright, as if they had recently been brush-cleaned.

"Get on the train, Turtle," said Nick firmly.

Nate grabbed Turtle by the arm. "Come on," he said.

Somewhere inside the train, a chime rang twice.

"This thing doesn't stop for long, and you're not getting out of that door there. It's locked now on this side. Come on," urged Nick. He grabbed Turtle's arm and pulled him onto the train. Had Nick not prodded him, he probably wouldn't have moved.

Another chime sounded and the doors hissed shut. Another hiss of air signaled that the brakes had let go. The train began to trundle down the tracks and pick up speed as it moved into the darkness.

Turtle stood, holding onto a leather hand strap, and stared intently out the window at the darkness.

"Guys, seriously. What is this? Is this a joke?"

"It's no joke. It's a train we use sometimes," said Nate.

"Like New Jersey Transit?" asked Turtle.

"Not quite. But it goes most places you need it to go," said Nate. Nick elbowed him to be quiet.

"Where are we going now?" asked Turtle.

"It stops at 69th Street, by the finish line."

"Is that how you keep winning races?"

"Sure. Our uncle showed us."

Nate and Nick sat down. In their shorts and gym shirts, they looked out of place amid the train's plush decor. Wicker chairs lined the entire car, each one bolted beneath the wide glass windows. Small oil lamps flickered above the seats, and a sign above the door said "Mytro." Turtle ran to the window to catch a glimpse of the tunnel, but, except for the bright red lights on the roof and the front headlight, it was completely dark outside.

"This is how we get As in gym," said Nate.

"By riding a secret train in the middle of Central Park?" yelled Turtle. Nate and Nick looked at each other and shrugged.

"Sure," they said in unison.

"But no one is supposed to know about this, Turtle. We could get in trouble," said Nick.

Turtle turned red with anger.

"This is not only crazy, it's cheating!" he blasted, his voice muffled by the rattling train and the rich velvet curtains hung along the clear glass windows. The whole train rocked side to side as they moved, and Turtle could tell they were moving fast.

"Sit down. Just wait," said Nick.

Nick didn't like Turtle as much as Nate did. Nate was into video games and computers—like Turtle—and Nick had a band and was into music. The two rarely played together, and Nick never sat with Turtle at lunch. Neither of them had ever been to Turtle's house, but he had been to theirs.

Turtle's house was too far, and he was embarrassed when he told people that he lived in Brooklyn, over the bridge from Manhattan. Living "in the city" was a big deal—it meant your family had money and you could ride cabs to school.

Some kids even had a driver to take them from their apartments to the front door of Manhattan Friends, where they all were in eighth grade. Nick and Nate lived in the city, and Turtle lived in Bay Ridge, two places that were only five miles apart, but as distant from each other as the earth to the moon.

"Are you going to tell, Turtle?" asked Nick.

Turtle took a deep breath. "No," he said. "I won't tell. But what is all this? Who runs it?"

"We don't know," said Nate. "Our uncle showed us a few stops and gave us a map. We use it to get around the city."

"Who owns it?" asked Turtle, but Nick was busy looking over Turtle's shoulder and Nate was standing up.

"Nobody," said Nate. "Nobody owns it, which is why it's so great."

The train began to slow.

"Here's our stop," said Nick.

He led Turtle off the train into another station. The walls were covered in gray-brown tile painted like duck feathers. The station name was "Central Park Mid."

They rushed past the wooden ticket counter—identical to the one in the previous station down to a matching "Closed" sign—and on through the door. A scattering of tickets swirled around their feet as they opened it.

On the other side, Turtle realized they were behind another rock and another stand of tall bushes. The door shut behind them, disappearing completely into the face of the enormous rock. This door was covered by a cluster of tall, old trees and more of the sweet-smelling greenery, but there was no path. They popped through and stood blinking in the sunlight. Nick and Nate started running.

"Come on!" hissed Nick. "Run faster. We need to work up a sweat."

"I'm already sweating like crazy," said Turtle. "That was intense."

"Pretty cool, huh?" asked Nate.

"Pretty cool," said Turtle.

A minute later, they were at the finish line and in the middle of the pack, an acceptable performance. On the walk back to school, Nick, Nate, and Turtle hung back.

"OK, guys. Now, you have to tell me how to get back on there. How did your uncle find it?"

"It's a long story," said Nate with a smile.

"And we need to ask our uncle before we tell it," said Nick.

CHAPTER TWO

The Map

Turtle ran with the Kincaids back to the school building where the track team, six boys in all, was just straggling into the locker room.

Going to Manhattan Friends was considered a privilege and an honor. Turtle had done exceedingly well on a scholarship test in fourth grade and so was able to gain that honor and privilege for free. His grades were excellent—all As except for a B in gym one year—but Turtle had almost no friends. He just didn't have much in common with very many there, and one kid he did like, Romain, transferred back to Switzerland when his parents were fired from their Wall Street jobs. Turtle relished the thought of speaking more with Nick and Nate, especially if it was about whatever he had just seen.

The Kincaids lived on Central Park West in a townhouse five times the size Turtle's grandmother's house. Turtle's one visit to their home was for their 13th birthday party. Their three-story, rich, dark chocolate cake had been decorated with pictures of the twins on each layer that were made of some kind of printed sugar. There was a picture of the twins as babies, then as 10-year-olds on the beach, then a snapshot of them a few years older standing near a castle. When Turtle turned 13, his grandmother had made him a cake from a box with butter frosting, and they blew out his candles and opened the few presents she could afford for him.

Turtle's parents died in a car accident north of the city when he was three. From that moment, all Turtle remembered was his grandmother and their little house in Bay Ridge. His parents were reduced to snapshots in an album that his grandmother sometimes took down from the shelf on rainy mornings. They would flip through the album and remember when they both had families.

After showering with the rest of the team, Turtle made his way into the rowdy locker room. Toweling off, he tried to look uninterested as the Kincaids talked about a video game they had been playing. He didn't interrupt them, waiting instead for the locker room to clear. There were four kids on the benches and a few by the water fountain. It was getting late—chauffeur-driven black cars were already pulling up to pick up the rich kids—and the track team began to clear out.

Nate looked over at Turtle and motioned for him to move closer. The overhead fan echoing in the locker room was loud enough to drown a whisper.

"Stay after," he breathed. "Wait a little."

Once the locker room was empty, Nick and Nate moved their bags over to Turtle's bench and sat down. The coach, Mr. Huff, was in his office with the door slightly ajar. He flexed one thick arm and went back to writing something.

"You're going to keep this a secret?" asked Nick. His face was set and serious. Turtle nodded.

"Seriously," said Nick.

"Yes, I will," said Turtle.

"I don't like this," said Nick. Nate shrugged, opened his backpack, and removed a piece of paper. He pulled on a thin black sweater and then a black blazer while Turtle looked the paper over. Nick was in a button-down shirt and black pants—the school uniform—but Turtle was already in jeans and a T-shirt for the ride home.

The page was about 14 inches square, and it looked like a photocopy of a photocopy, faded and crumpled. It was a map, covered with small squiggles and lines. They spread it out on the bench, smoothing it down and avoiding the wet spots.

"I can't give you this one, but this is a Map. Without this, you can't get onto the train. You'd get lost," said Nate.

Turtle gulped. The thought of roaring through those tunnels, alone and lost, frightened him. He knelt down on one knee for a closer look. The map was a reprint of something much older and hand-drawn. It showed all of Manhattan—a long cigar laced with avenues—Brooklyn and Queens sticking out below and a bit of New Jersey and Staten Island looking like a mini-South America. To first-time visitors, the New York City Subway map already looked like a mess of spaghetti with lines running up and down from Brooklyn into Harlem to the north. But that was nothing compared to this wild map.

Lines crossed the map frantically, some gray, some lighter, some in dark black. Some lines had faded away; you could barely tell where they began and ended. But the stops that would be most helpful to Nick and Nate, the stops along Central Park and near the school, had been drawn over in blue ink to make them a bit clearer. The names of stations were written in a tiny, careful hand, and it looked like some lines even connected with Brooklyn and New Jersey over (or under) the water. The lines disappeared off the page, and in some of the corners, there was evidence of more stations farther into New Jersey and even a line that shot straight out into the North Atlantic Ocean.

In the upper right corner was one word, plainly written in pen:

MYTRO

"Mytro," said Turtle.

Nate pointed to a spot on the map—labeled "Friends Meeting Hall"—and then pointed to a door a few feet away from where they stood marked "STAFF ONLY." Written on the sign in black paint, now faded, was the number 13.

"That's the local station, right here. You go in past the boiler room. This building used to be a Quaker meeting hall and they built the school up around it when they decided to start teaching kids. So it's called a meeting hall and not a school. These maps are crazy old," said Nate.

"The door is actually built into the far wall of the boiler room. The problem is they started locking the boiler room when they thought someone was sneaking in to smoke," he said.

"That was you?" asked Turtle, recalling a witch hunt led by Mr.

Huff and the bald, pudgy principal, Mr. Quigley. Mr. Huff had told the team that if they wanted to hang out in the boiler room so much, they could run laps in it, which they did—in the heat and the dirt—for almost an hour. Then the janitor, Mr. Goudas, locked it permanently with a huge silver padlock.

"We were coming out, not going in. That was the best four weeks because we could get from our house to here on the Mytro in like a minute. We could sleep in all we wanted."

"The entrances to the Mytro ... are they all doors?" asked Turtle, thinking about the rock.

"No, they're not. The station near our Mom's house is behind a brick wall. Sometimes they're just door doors, you know? But that's when they're completely hidden, no one can see them. The trick is to find the ways in."

"Where do the stations come from?" asked Turtle.

"Who knows? My uncle said that if they tore down this building, the station would disappear, but if you build up another wall and put a door into it, the station comes back. At least it's supposed to."

Turtle nodded, but he had no idea what Nate was talking about—which the look on his face clearly showed.

"You'll get it pretty soon," said Nate. "It's hard to understand until, you know, you ride it a few times. Think of it like magic, but my uncle says it isn't. He says it has something to do with wormholes, two spots that open up in space or whatever. He's been trying to figure these things out."

"So you have a station in your house?" asked Turtle.

"No, it's in a deli down the street. The deli guy knows about it. It's in his basement. We wake up, go get a soda, and then go downstairs to get to school. Now we have to pop up behind the school, in Bums, instead of right here."

Bums was an alley behind the school where the upperclassmen smoked. Turtle had been there once and was chased off by the football team's quarterback, a moose of a kid named Harvey Klawe.

Nick tapped Nate on the shoulder. Mr. Huff was shuffling behind his office door. "Here he comes." Nate folded the map and put it quickly away.

Mr. Huff walked out, drinking a diet soda. "What are you guys doing out here? Go home," he said.

"Video games, Mr. Huff," said Nate.

Mr. Huff grunted and said, "You guys could probably get a few more miles in instead of playing whatever video games you're playing these days."

"Yes, sir," said Nick, and he grabbed Nate by the arm and led him out of the locker room. Nick reached back to take his duffel bag, and they nodded their good-byes. The boys barreled through the back doors, around the school, and out into the street.

After the quiet of the locker room, Fifth Avenue sounded like a circus. Horns honked and people passed in a blur. A bicycle messenger roared past them blowing a whistle, and the air smelled like rain. Turtle marveled at the streets, wondering where the snaking lines of the train—the Mytro—were hidden.

"There are tunnels under there?"

Nate shook his head. "If there were, they'd have found them by now. Just doors and stations. No tunnels."

Turtle looked at the Kincaid twins. He half expected them to start laughing, to tell him it was all a gag, that the short run in the park was some forgotten part of the subway they opened up for a special occasion.

"This isn't anything you can talk about. I don't know how you got in after us, but it's not good," said Nick. "You just be careful."

"Why?" asked Turtle.

"It's instant travel," said Nate. "You can get on at the Mytro here and get off in Staten Island a minute later. You can move almost anything through the Mytro. I think you used to be able to go anywhere in the world, but something happened, and it's much harder to get to different places now."

They started walking to the park. "Can I ride it home?" asked Turtle.

"Not until you get a map. You can't go anywhere without a map. We'll talk to my uncle," said Nate.

Nick was already walking ahead of them as they strode into the park again. Turtle's eyes strayed to the spot where he knew the Central Park Mid station was hidden, a few yards from where they entered the park.

"Do you steer it? Tell it where to go?"

"You think about where you want to go—but you have to be

careful. You have to know where you want to go before you get on because it keeps going if you're not sure where you want to get off."

Questions raced through his head. Who built the Mytro? Why did their uncle know so much? Who else knew?

"Listen, I have an idea," said Nate. "Tomorrow's Friday. Ask your grandma if you can stay over at our house. Then we can go see my uncle. Here's my number. Call me." Nate scribbled it on a piece of ripped homework and handed it over. Turtle took it and stuffed it into his jeans.

"Very cool," said Turtle and he made his way through the park to the real subway.

CHAPTER THREE

Cierra La Puerta

Instead of taking his regular subway stop near the school, Turtle decided he needed to clear his head. Walking, he passed the secret Central Park Mid entrance—now blocked by two kids with skateboards doing tricks on a nearby rail and a thin man with glasses watched them, puzzled, from a park bench. Ten blocks later, he passed the station they exited to beat everyone on the track team. Ten blocks was almost a mile, which meant that maybe whoever had built the Mytro placed stations in the same positions as the current, "real" subway stations. It was a parallel network, but one much bigger and much more mysterious.

His nerves were humming. Today was a day of firsts. For the first time, he got to talk to Nick and Nate for more than five minutes about something other than schoolwork, and it was the first time they'd trusted him with something big. It was also the first time he rode the Mytro.

Being a nerd at Manhattan Friends wasn't bad, but it wasn't great for his social life. Being invited for a sleepover at the Kincaids' was a big deal. Then there was the Mytro. It was so much to process that he had, in what seemed like only a few seconds, travelled a mile through Central Park.

It just so happened that Turtle's hobby was magic. He liked to practice card tricks and had a whole drawer full of simple tricks—fake thumbs for performing scarf illusions, trick coins for the shell game, and a number of big books on street magic.

The three steps of any magic trick are the Declaration, the Turn, and the Prestige. The Declaration is the part where you show the audience what you're about to do. The Turn is actually doing it, and then the Prestige is the trick, the thing that makes everyone gasp. The Mytro was all Prestige.

He took out a quarter and practiced a coin walk, popping the coin over each of his knuckles and into his hand. His tricks made him a hit at family parties. Though he knew that most of the time they humored him, some of his tricks surprised everyone, even those who had seen them countless times. He had gotten really good at picking pockets—brushing up against members of the audience and grabbing a watch or a wallet.

He liked computers and he was also into cryptology, from the simplest substitution ciphers to more complex, computerized protection systems. He was fascinated by prime numbers, and he kept a notebook of primes he could find in his textbooks. It was a strange hobby, but his father had been a mathematician at New York University, and his grandmother still had a stack of books and notes he had used during his time there. Turtle loved to open them and inhale the rich scent of old paper and something slightly floral— maybe a whiff of his mother's perfume or some kind of incense? It brought him back to a happier time, a time full of sunlight that he could barely remember when his mother and father were still alive.

He sped up a bit and then paused by the entrance to the Central Park South station. The path in the grass was obvious now, if you knew where to look. The jackhammer still burred across the street.

Careful not to attract attention, Turtle approached the tall bushes and parted them again. He reached out and touched the rock. Behind it, somewhere deep in the stone, he felt the train roar into the station.

All it would take was a slight push and he'd be inside, but he froze, thinking of being lost in the endless tunnels. He'd be traveling then, without a goal and without any idea of where he was going to end up—if he ever came back out at all. Turtle imagined riding the train forever, like a ghost haunting the tunnels. He didn't even have a snack in his backpack, let alone enough water to survive lost in the tunnels for long.

The door ceased vibrating, so Turtle pressed his ear to the stone.

On the inside, someone (or something) started pounding. He heard a faint voice, a girl's voice. Then Turtle heard the pounding again.

Someone needed help.

He pushed the stone face and the wind began to suck him in. He held onto the bushes and pushed harder. Suddenly, barreling out of the Mytro door was a girl about his age with long black hair. Her green eyes were wide with fear and she pushed past Turtle and out into the park.

"*Ayúdame!*" she yelled. "*Cierra la puerta!*" Behind her he saw two men exit the train and race towards them.

"What?" he yelled. The girl looked at him and then back at the men on the platform.

"Close the door!" she screamed. He let go and it whooshed shut. The girl sat down on the grass, panting.

"Please," she said. "I need your help."

CHAPTER FOUR

The Exchange Student

The girl was very pretty. She had tanned skin and high, strong cheekbones. She wore jeans, a gray hoodie, and a backpack that bulged nearly to the breaking point. The knees of her jeans were smudged with dirt and grass. She looked up at Turtle.

"*Donde estamos?* Where are we?" she asked. She held out a hand so Turtle could help her up.

Turtle paused for a moment, wiped his hands on his pants, and lifted her off the grass. She stood a good half head taller than Turtle.

"You're in New York," said Turtle. "This is Manhattan. Central Park."

"This is where I wanted to be," she said, brushing herself off. "Thank you," she said, with a hint of an accent. She smelled like some kind of flower, a scent that Turtle recognized from somewhere but couldn't place.

She looked around her, catching her breath. The fear Turtle had seen in her was fading. Finally she turned back to Turtle.

"I'm Turtle. I mean Paul. People call me Turtle, though."

"My name is Agata. Agata Llorente." She pronounced it Yo-rent-ay, rolling the R slightly. A necklace slipped out of her shirt—a leather string with a jagged-looking coin made of dull brass or copper, a bit green on the edges. She pushed it back under her shirt as she straightened up.

"Is there somewhere we can go? Can we get away from here?"

Behind her, Turtle heard noises from the other side of the stone.

Those men were shouting to be let out. They pounded for a while and then stopped.

Turtle looked around. A crowd of tourists was standing near the bench, taking pictures with the rock as a background.

The Mytro knows when people are looking at it, thought Turtle.

"They were following me and they finally found me," Agata said. "I don't know why they didn't come out."

"I think this door only opens one way," said Turtle. "It was just lucky I opened it when I did. Who's following you? Why?"

"It's a long story. Let's walk. Where are you going?"

"I'm going home. To my grandmother's."

"Can I come? Say I'm a friend from school? Say I'm a ... what do you call them? Exchange?"

"Exchange student?" Turtle offered.

"Exactly. I'm an exchange student."

Turtle looked at the girl and then at the door. The men behind it had guns—he had seen them in their hands before the door swooshed shut. They were angry at her, and she was in trouble. But why?

Her gaze followed his and then returned, her eyes pleading. "Please, Turtle. I need help. I need to get to a safe place. I'll try to explain on the way."

Her breathing was normal now, but the look on her face—panic, fear, the need to escape—convinced him he needed to help. It was, after all, not every day that he met a girl falling out of an invisible subway system in the middle of Central Park.

"Who are you? Where did you come from?" he asked warily, though he was already sure he would help her.

"I'm from Barcelona. I'm 14. My father is lost somewhere behind that door. Someone kidnapped my mother. Those men are trying to find me now. They'll find another door and then they'll be after me. Did you see they have guns?"

Turtle gulped and nodded. "I know what's back there. It's the Mytro. But they're after *us*, now," he said. "I'll get you out of here, but we should go to the police."

"Where will we lead them? To the Mytro? Police won't believe us."

Turtle stood thinking. Agata shook her head impatiently and

took Turtle's arm, leading him away from the door as casually as if they were going for a stroll. It felt strange and wildly exciting. It was the first time a girl had taken his arm. *Maybe kids walked arm in arm in Spain?* thought Turtle.

Softly, behind the stone door, Turtle heard the train rattle back in, but soon they were on the main path and headed to the N subway stop. They walked past the old man on the bench who looked at Turtle and the girl quizzically, confused as to where they had come from and what the commotion had been about. He nodded off as they passed, perhaps exhausted by the hard job of being curious.

"Do you ride the Mytro often?" she asked when they were farther down the path.

"Today's my first day," said Turtle. "I just found out about it."

"So we're in the same ship."

"The same ship?"

"Same boat? This is my first time," she said. "So we are in the same boat."

They walked to the subway stop at the foot of the park.

"If we act natural, your grandmother won't care, right?" said Agata.

"I don't even know," said Turtle. "She's really nice, but this is a pretty special case."

"There is only one way to find out," she said, smiling, and she let him lead her down the stairs into the subway.

CHAPTER FIVE

Rattling in the Dark

They worked forever. They did not sleep. They did not have eyes, so they did not need to close them.

The rattling in the dark was their song, the noise of their birth and the harbinger of their twilight. Here on Earth it was always rattling. Men had made the Mytro in their own image, and they had decidedly closed imaginations. If the Mytro had a shape, they knew it better than anyone, but they were forced, by men, by the Mytro, to maintain the charade.

They were called Nayzuns—the Nameless Ones. But they had names and they knew the Mytro like a governess knows her charge.

The Nayzuns were made to know the shape, to build the shape, to complete the shape. In their dark world, the rails of the Mytro were not rails at all, but strings of energy connecting each living thing through the impossibility of space. They lived here in a massive Hangar at the edge of the Earth System. There were other systems, far away, but this one was theirs.

Now they all lifted their heads away from their work, like stalks of wheat bobbing away from a gust of wind. They glowed, gently and all at once, when something caught their attention. A few hours before, they had heard the rails tell of strangers on the Mytro. They had been listening for the strangers, and they had finally heard them, somewhere down the line. The strangers had broken a train with their weapons. If there was one thing that couldn't be condoned on the Mytro, it was an act of destruction. The Mytro was angry.

The broken train lurched into the Hangar, into their home.

A car with shattered windows slowed to a halt by 411's work area. Glass tinkled out of the metal frame and onto the ground, disappearing into the darkness. The lights inside the car were winking on and off, the oil-pumping mechanism that fed them failing intermittently, the tongues of flame dimming and rising.

411 was the train foreman. He called the younger ones to him, and they shuffled out of the dark.

411 knew that the oil tank had been ruptured somewhere and that oil was leaking onto the ground, the smell rich like dead, decaying leaves. Although 411 did not know this, the Mytro on Earth was built to calm the humans. It was a system designed to soothe the primitive minds of those who rode it. To show them the Mytro as it really was, a skein of light that connected the universe, would force them to face their own insignificance. The trains were easier.

The light from the car's front headlight was useless in the Hangar. The vaults of this room disappeared into darkness. No light penetrated the darkest quarters of the huge bay, and no thing with eyes had ever seen what was hidden there.

Whether the room even had a ceiling, really, was still in doubt. When the Nayzuns were created, they fell to the ground and began to work. When the Nayzuns died, the Mytro took them to a place where there was no mourning. But the Nayzuns rarely died these days. They were too busy, and they had not had a young one in many years. Instead, the Mytro simply brought them back in time to live out a few more years. It was a cruel fate—to work forever and never die—but the Nayzuns knew no other one.

411 had been working on Earth longer than most. His number was quite small as he had been created early in the history of the Mytro on this planet. He had seen it grow here on Earth, and he had seen the Mytro fail and disappear. He had seen it hidden away, then rediscovered. He loved it like his child, for he could have no

children. The men above had no idea what sort of power they had right under their plodding feet.

411 looked down the track that was not a track. The train with the shattered windows swayed as the Mytro's machinery pitched it off the tracks. The car settled with a thump on 411's own small set of side tracks where it would be fixed. The younger Nayzuns were already hard at work, pulling out the broken windows and bringing new ones from the storage area. If there had been more light, they would have looked like gigantic, long-limbed spiders scrabbling over the varnished wood of the Mytro car, their pointed fingers brushing glass into dark holes near the work area and the pads of their hands softly scanning the surface of the train for imperfections.

The rails began to speak. *There were men on the tracks now. They had an incomplete map, so they would soon be swallowed.*

411 knew what this meant. Fools on the rails were dangerous. If they kept riding, they would break the tracks, and the Mytro would roar and erase them.

The Mytro was increasingly angry now, and cruel. Once, it tore down whole cities on a whim, brought floods and earthquakes where it could. It had, after all, the right-of-way.

411 remembered the Mytro, long ago, when men knew nothing of its powers. He remembered the first men that were sent howling down her tunnels.

The Mytro was their history entire. Their ancient stories, passed from father to child long ago, spoke of the Mytro as the Way. She appeared to them as a shining thread through the darkness, the one confirmation that the universe had a reason. There was matter and there was the Mytro. She had many names and many creatures claimed to control her, but now she was alone in her majesty.

The Nayzuns were her workers, bent to her. She fed them. They did not eat as humans did, but what the Mytro fed them was sufficient, and the others often brought nourishment on her rails that they could not get here. The Mytro turned them into beasts of burden, useful in all ways and specifically designed to survive only under its care.

So were they slaves? 411 did not think so, but now his way of life was being threatened. The humans were back.

Now, for the second time in a century, humans wanted to take the Mytro and have it for themselves. These men had maps, and they had knowledge of the Mytro that was dangerously incomplete. Their hunt would imperil everyone, including the Nayzuns.

The men were in the tunnels now, their anger and fear and desire cascading through the skeins like a terrible song plucked on a spider's web. He signaled to 227 farther down the tunnel to move away. The train barreled through, the Mytro complaining in its voice of rattling, squealing, and hissing steam. The Mytro spoke through the machines. It spoke through steel and brass and wood. The Mytro was angry.

The Nayzuns swarmed the train. In the dark, the scents of the intruders were as clear as the smell of fire. The girl's was sharp and floral. The men smelled like anger and fear. Over it all was gunpowder, the propellant that had caused the Mytro so much trouble in the past. 411 could still remember the day a dead human rolled into the Hangar. The Nayzuns had swarmed the train and then froze. They wanted so much to touch this human, a woman who had been stabbed, but they could not. The Mytro wanted them to have no contact with the humans. Humans had diseases, they had death, and, more importantly, humans had free will. The Nayzuns let the car roll back into the dark, and the Mytro swallowed the woman, taking her far from the Hangar, into parts of the skein they had never seen.

The girl's scent intrigued 411. He knew the girl was in grave danger, but he could do nothing. He walked down the center of the car, feeling for damage. The terrible smell of gunpowder was deeper here. The younger Nayzuns deferred to him and seemed to melt away as he passed. 411 was a sub-conductor. He could stop the trains at any time, but he knew it was not his place. The humans owned this stretch of track, and they would have to solve this problem themselves.

By the headlight of the shattered train, 411 looked like a stick man drawn by a lazy child, a mantis with long arms and longer legs, stretched out taut as a guitar string. His face, if he could be said to have a face, was one with his neck and he had only a mouth. His visage was horrific and angelic at once. He and his kind had been mistaken for demons for centuries. One man, long ago, fell down into the Mytro and returned to Earth, telling stories of demons manning the bellows of hell. After that, the Nayzuns rarely left the Hangar.

But something was drawing 411 to this girl. Was it her scent? Was it the crying of the rails when she was traveling? The rails felt a need to protect her. 411 stopped to listen. The Mytro would tell him what to do.

Suddenly, a wind blew up along the tracks and ruffled the Nayzuns like a gale. The rails again.

Find her, the rails sang.

411 spoke: *I am at your command. But do I go to the humans?*

Find her, the rails sang. *She is important to us. She has the Keys.*

411 wondered why the Mytro wanted her. Was the Mytro looking for sacrifices? 411 thought of the man he was hiding. The Mytro didn't yet know about this man, miraculously. Were the two connected?

411 whistled to 227 and the other Nayzun approached.

Something is the matter, said 411, his voice the whisper of a wire brush on steel.

227, an older Nayzun, had been repairing the tunnel walls with a dark material that glittered with starlight. 227 nodded.

What will you do? asked 227. *You must bring his Key to us.*

I will go up the tracks. Keep working. I will return.

Most Nayzuns never saw the inside of the stations. Only the old ones could do that, and that was where 411 had met the man and where 411 learned of his power. The young Nayzuns were relegated to simple work like tunnel repair, cleaning, and the like. They never felt the comfort of a cool wicker chair or a journey that wasn't predicated on their work.

227 turned toward the wall abruptly and continued to patch the tunnel walls. Nayzuns rarely stood on ceremony or engaged in small talk. Everything they could have said they had said. Their race was old and quiet as a night-shackled forest.

411 stood against the wall and waited for the next train to come. He hitched himself to it, spinning behind it like a wraith, and rattled through the dark of the tunnels to where he had heard the shots. He didn't have to ask the Mytro to take him there. The Mytro knew where to take him.

CHAPTER SIX

The Subway

Agata sat with Turtle on the N train as it ratcheted out of the tunnel and over the East River into Brooklyn. The train was almost empty, so they both got seats, Agata by the window and Turtle next to her.

He had led her to his regular subway stop and paid for her ticket. Now that they were far from the door in the rock, Agata was noticeably more relaxed.

She was looking out at the city, a small smile on her lips. The rails clattered below them, and somewhere, in the back of the train car, a woman was loudly reading from some kind of political book. She had gotten on at Canal Street and was now reaching a fever pitch, talking about the economy and jobs and the Bronx Zoo.

"Be quiet, already!" someone yelled from across the train, and the woman, her face reddening, went quiet.

"Is that the Statue of Liberty?" Agata asked, pointing to a small green spot on the horizon that was slowly becoming clearer as they came out of the tunnel.

Turtle nodded. "Yep. It's green, which is funny because it used to be golden. The air changed it, basically. We're on the Manhattan Bridge. That's the Brooklyn Bridge, there."

The Brooklyn Bridge looked striking in the afternoon, all spires and cables and dark stone. The styling, Turtle noted, was very similar to the Mytro stations he had seen. Maybe they were made at the same time? The bridge had two large pilings and a span held up by delicate-looking steel ropes, spun, his grandmother had told him, somewhere in Pennsylvania by a man who had become an expert at braiding metal.

"It's a very beautiful city," said Agata. "Barcelona is beautiful, too, but not in the same way. Barcelona is older, definitely."

"I guess New York is pretty. Plenty of people like it, but I haven't really been anywhere else. Why did you come here?" asked Turtle.

"I'd never been to New York," she said. "This is my first time on the Mytro. My uncle Ernesto said he had a friend here, so I came."

"Who is the friend?"

"I will have to check my notebook. A man named Kincaid, I believe. I knew him when I was very small. Uncle Ernesto said if we were separated, I was to come here and find his friend. He would help me."

"Kincaid? And he lives in New York?"

"Yes," he said.

The hair on the back of Turtle's neck suddenly prickled.

"This is totally weird," said Turtle, "but I think I may know the Kincaid family."

"It's a small land," she said, smiling. "Is that right?"

"Small world," he corrected her, but she was already looking out the window, deep in thought.

Agata and Turtle sat quietly for a bit. Turtle thought about the subway they were riding and how it existed—for want of a better word—and how it came to be. And how different it was from the Mytro, the thing that—for want of a better word—did not exist.

"I'm tired of invisible trains," said Agata. "Tell me about New York."

Turtle had read a lot about the subway. He cleared his throat and began to tell Agata about a subterranean world that actually did exist, that did have real tunnels and stations. He told her about the New York subway.

He wasn't sure if Barcelona had a subway (she assured him it did), and so he began telling her what he knew. He told Agata that builders began the first New York line in about 1870 when bankers built a pneumatic tunnel that connected city hall in downtown Manhattan with Murray Street.

"Where's that?" asked Agata. Turtle held up his right hand, his forefingers pointed toward the floor, and pointed to the nail of his middle finger.

"Imagine Manhattan looks like my arm. Up by my elbow is Harlem and Yonkers and down here, by my thumb, is what they call Alphabet City. Down at the tip is downtown. Right where I'm pointing is about where city hall is."

"Downtown is where the towers were?"

Turtle nodded. She seemed to shiver at the thought of the World Trade Center.

"The first tunnel was really short," said Turtle. "It was about 300 feet long, and it was open for only about three years. Way back then most of the city was at the tip of the island and maybe a little bit across the river in Brooklyn. The river was really dangerous, and they had people who would take you by boat over from Brooklyn—where they had farms, way back then—to Manhattan. They had to build a bridge because there were so many boats on the water that lots of people were getting knocked overboard. They built the subway so people wouldn't get smashed under all the horses and carriages that ran through the city back then."

From this tiny seed the subway system grew to a massive 656 miles long with 468 stations ranging from northern Manhattan and the Bronx down to Coney Island. Turtle often sat in his room looking at the subway map and plotting out the fastest and simplest ways to get from his house to distant stations. He had heard that once a kid had ridden all the lines on the subway in a few weeks, riding it through the night and stopping in every single station. His grandmother, who usually encouraged and supported his interests and hobbies, had forbidden him from trying the same trip.

The subways were clean and well lit, although his grandmother told him of times when the trains were covered in graffiti and smelled like a sewer. Now the trains eased into the station, the doors opened, and the announcements played—"Doors closing. Please stand clear of the closing doors"—and the train buzzed off into the darkness with an electric hum.

He was finished by the time they came to 36th Street in Brooklyn, about ten minutes later. "You told me about your trains, so let me tell you about mine," said Agata.

Agata began to speak, her voice low and quiet over the rattle-clack of the wheels on the steel rails. She was a careful storyteller, and she tried to be as thorough as possible. When Turtle began to look confused, she'd back up and start again. He loved to listen to her.

CHAPTER SEVEN

Silencio

For years, no one knew what Agata's father did in his attic. He would wake in the morning, eat breakfast with his family (a hardboiled egg, a piece of dry toast, and coffee), and then climb the stairs in their three-story home to begin his work. He would come down at five o'clock, just as the streets around their building off the bustling Rambla district began to liven with commuters.

Years ago, her father had been a professor at Cambridge. He had taught physics and studied stellar phenomena—that's all Agata's mother had ever told her.

They lived on a small street lined with tiny grocery stores that sold sparkling wine and thinly sliced ham that her mother, a vegetarian, never bought. Their home had been in the family for almost a century, and they owned the majority of it, renting out the bottom two floors to tenants and keeping the top two for themselves. The attic was connected to the third floor by a thin spiral staircase, so when her father ordered new computer equipment or office furniture, they had to lift it using a special crane outside the window.

Her father seldom talked about what he did for a living. Even Agata's American mother knew nothing of his work. When asked, she would smile and shrug. "He does research," she'd say. "Special research." Agata's mother, Claire, was used to keeping her husband's work a secret. She taught Agata English and her father taught her Spanish and Catalan. They had never been to the U.S., but they had many friends who visited from abroad.

Agata went to the English Academy in Barcelona and was an only child. Like her father, she kept to herself and read most nights until very late, her room bathed in the warm glow of a small lamp her father bought her. It was shaped like an old passenger train from a very long time ago, and the light poured from its tiny colored-glass windows and through the front headlight. When her father was especially immersed in his work, she rarely saw him and instead heard him creaking about upstairs as he moved from computer to computer, checking printouts and consulting thick, dusty books that came almost daily to the house from the national library.

A week before she had tumbled out of the rock and into Turtle's life, her father began acting strangely. He never came down for breakfast, asking instead for food to be sent up. But he never ate. Breakfast trays would lie at the foot of the steps for most of the day, and when Agata came home, she would bring them down to her mother who would scrape the uneaten food into the garbage.

Her mother said nothing, but the strain in her face was clear. Some afternoons, Agata could hear her mother crying in the kitchen while she was reading on the couch. Going in to see her, Agata would find her sitting at the table with a cup of coffee, her eyes red but a smile on her face.

"What is it, *mi cielo*?" she would ask. *My heaven.* That's what her father called her, and sometimes her mother used it too. The sound made Agata shiver a little.

"Daddy's just been busy," she said. "Don't worry. I get worried when he doesn't eat. I made him eat two sandwiches yesterday when you were asleep."

Her father was always very private, but this week was different. The house was far quieter than it ever was, and she hadn't seen her father for days. He didn't usually hide away for so long.

Even when Agata knew her father should have been home, she felt like he was gone. The house was just empty. It was the feeling you got when you knew a television was on somewhere in the house, but this was the opposite—something missing, something turned off.

She would walk through the door and call out to him, but she heard nothing and was too scared to go upstairs to disturb him. So she would eat something—a piece of toast with tomato or some cheese—and wait for him to come down at about four o'clock. He usually did. On the days he didn't come down she felt an icy chill, as if he were well and truly gone, as if his attic was empty and he would never return.

When she came home after school two days before, she knew something was different. The house was still, and the clock in the living room ticked explosively as she listened for her father's footsteps upstairs. Four o'clock came and went and then four thirty. She called up to her father and left a message, her voice echoing in the house. No reply. Complete silence. She sat down at the kitchen table to wait and watched the sun creep across the window and cast longer and longer shadows on the kitchen counter. It was getting late. Her mother came home, her face pale with worry, but, finally, at eight o'clock her father thumped down the stairs into the kitchen, his thin face flushed with excitement.

Agata's father looked like a stretched-out version of Agata. They both had the same skin color, the same color hair, the same green eyes—though his were hidden behind smudged glasses, a prescription so strong that his eyes looked like two floating fish. That night he and her mother drank a bottle of Cava at dinner, and, although it was clear he wouldn't be able to talk about what he had done, he was obviously quite excited.

The next day, her father was gone again. She called up: silence. She called his cell phone. It rang and rang and then dropped to his automated voicemail, a robotic voice reciting the digits of his phone number. She was tired of wondering.

Although he had never forbidden her from coming upstairs, it seemed like he never wanted to be disturbed. She could never tell why; her father was a kind, quiet man and rarely grew angry or upset. He seemed to cherish silence and privacy in his work, so she respected that. But that day, Agata finally decided to mount the stairs. Her mother was not home—she was out at the market and left a note and an egg salad sandwich in the kitchen for her—so Agata slowly took the spiral stairs one step at a time, calling out to her father as she went.

When she reached the top, she found the office in wild disarray. There were papers everywhere, and books lay open on their backs like gutted fish. All the computers were off, except for one, and it was driving the printer to pump out page after page of gibberish. Open on her father's central desk, bathed in sunlight from the open window, was a sheaf of yellow paper pinned together with an old rusted staple. On the front, in Spanish, it read "Mytro, Vias Catalonias." Under another, newer, map was a sheaf labeled "Mytro El Mundo." Next to it was a coin on a leather string, or something that looked like a coin. It had one serrated edge, like a sharp knife, and a curved edge. There were strange, small markings punched into the metal. Next to this, folded over once, was a note, which she picked up. The paper was heavy in her hand and she could tell it was from a stationery set she had purchased her father at the Mercado one Christmas. It was handmade and flecked with loose blue strings. The woman at the stall had said it was made of old blue jeans. She folded the note open and read.

It was written to her mother and said, in her father's ornate Spanish:

Claire, Beloved,

It is my hope that you will not have to read this, but if you do, understand that I am safe but it will take a long while for me to return. I have these many months been researching something that once belonged to our family and went missing, and I believe I have found it again.

Please take these items and keep them safe. They are keys to my discovery, and there may be people looking for them now that I have completed most of my research. Keep them with you at all times—don't simply leave them in the house. I want you to understand I am in no danger, and it is my belief that you and Agata will also be safe. Speak to no one about this and await further contact.

Hernando

When her mother returned, Agata showed her the note and the items. That night, even though it had been years since she slept in her parents' bed, she curled up next to her crying mother as they tried to sleep.

CHAPTER EIGHT

The Hill of Winds

The next morning, the air went out of their lives. Agata had no idea what to do.

"Where is he?" Agata asked. Her mother shrugged.

"I don't know, *bambina*. I honestly don't," said her mother, her eyes filling with tears as Agata crossed the room and took her into her small arms. "I promise we will find him," she said. "Your uncle Ernesto is looking. Don't worry."

"Did he say he knows where Dad is?"

Her mother shook her head and looked down into the swirls of milk in her coffee. She usually drank it black, but now she was drinking decaf with milk. *Maybe she didn't want to be awake as much,* thought Agata.

Agata moved through the house in a haze, getting her bag ready for school, collecting her papers from her desk. She paused at the stairs to her father's room. Maybe he would suddenly move up there. Maybe she would hear the telltale creak of his chair or his nervous, small cough, a cough that always used to annoy her but now she missed desperately. Maybe she would hear the clicking of a pen between his teeth as he sat thinking or staring out the attic window into the courtyard behind the house. But none of that happened. It was completely quiet.

Her mother gave Agata the map and coin to hold when she went to school. She didn't want them in the house, she explained.

Agata walked to school, and the day went by in a blur. She could not pay attention, and her teachers didn't call on her. Her math teacher, Mrs. Torres, took her aside after class.

"*Todo bien?*" she asked. "Is everything OK?"

"Everything is fine. My father and mother are having problems," said Agata. She trusted Mrs. Torres, but not enough to talk about what was going on.

"Is there anything I can do? Do you need to talk to the counselor?"

"*No, gracias.* My uncle is helping us. It will be OK."

Mrs. Torres gave her a brief hug. "*Se fuerte, Agata.*"

When class ended and Agata went out to the street, her mother was not there. She waited for ten minutes, twenty. She called, but no one answered. A chill ran through her and she was near tears, shaking. She sucked it back down, and, finally, she walked home.

She took out the long skeleton key that unlocked the main bolt and turned it in the front door. It clicked open and the door swung inward.

"Mama?" she called.

Silence.

"Mama?" Still nothing. The house was empty and quiet. Looking around, she began to notice the mess.

Her mother was gone. Most of the house had been ransacked. Her mother's purse was ripped open on the floor, her makeup and wallet littering the wood planks. Papers spilled down the stairs from the attic and covered the halls upstairs. Most of the rooms had been searched, the drawers ripped open and flipped, emptied of the contents and further desecrated by boots and knives. Books lay in wild disarray in her room, and her train lamp was broken, the ceramic shattered and the bulb a small pile of broken white glass.

She went from room to room, looking for any sign of who had done this. It was like a nightmare, and for a moment she thought she would pinch herself to try to wake up. Instead, she ran the serrated edge of her father's coin against the soft skin below her throat, but aside from a sharp pain and a red mark, nothing changed. This wasn't a dream, she decided. It was a nightmare.

She called her uncle's number and got his voicemail. She decided to go and find him.

Agata's uncle Ernesto, her father's older and only brother, lived outside Barcelona, so she quickly took her backpack and some clothes and rode the bus out to his large home in the outskirts. He was an art restorer, unmarried, and he spent many Sundays at her home arguing with her father about literature, art, and philosophy. The bus ride passed in a blur. She again tried to call her mother, her father, then Ernesto. Finally her phone died, and she nearly burst into tears. She walked the kilometer to Ernesto's house, and he answered the door. He looked almost like her father—skinnier, maybe, and with a little less hair. But there were her father's warm brown eyes, her father's dark hair. It was all she could do not to scream. He ushered her in, hugging her tightly.

"There you are," he said. "I wanted to go to the city to find you, but someone ruined my car engine. I was about to take a bus."

"My mother and father are gone. They were taken," said Agata.

"Don't worry, you're safe here. We'll find them both," he said. "There are a number of people looking for your father and mother. They're also watching me. Someone didn't want me to leave here. Are you OK? Did your father leave anything? A clue?"

"I'm fine. I'm fine. All I have are two things he left for my mother, some old papers and a coin."

"What papers?" asked Ernesto.

"I looked over the notes and they didn't make any sense. Something about an old train," she said.

Ernesto nodded.

"It's a very old train. Your father was researching it. He contacted me earlier this week and told me to keep my eye open if anything happened at the house. I hadn't heard anything from him for a while, so I called him. He called back, very distressed, and told me he couldn't talk. He said you would be coming to see me today, so tell me exactly what happened."

She recounted the night her father disappeared, her mother's muted reaction, and the break-in.

"Mother is gone and the house is a mess. They were looking for something. Was it these things?" asked Agata.

Her uncle thought for a minute. "This is your father's?" he asked, and he reached out to touch the leather cord around her neck. "This is the coin he left you?"

She nodded. He stared at it in awe.

"That must be it," he marveled when she tucked it back under her shirt. "This must be what they're after. Come to my office. There is something we must discuss."

Her uncle brought her into his office and told her to sit, then he brought her a cup of *horchata* and a sandwich and gave her a tissue to wipe her eyes.

"Everything is fine," he said. "Your father is in no danger as long as you have that around your neck. Your mother as well. Whatever is going on, it's all about something your father was working on—has been working on for a long time."

"How do you know?"

"Let me explain. Eat first."

Ernesto's study was as spartan as her father's was cluttered. A few pictures hung on the wall—her uncle and her family sitting at a picnic table at the beach before she was born, a diploma in fine arts from the *Real Academia de Bellas Artes de San Carlos de Valencia*, a picture of his fiancée who died of leukemia when Agata was still a baby. He had never become engaged again and lived alone, working on art restoration projects around the world.

"I'm going to explain a few very strange things to you, and I hope you will understand that I am not lying or playing a joke. Your father and I have been protecting a very important secret since we were your age, when our *abuela*, your great-grandmother, told us of it."

Ernesto began.

In 1823 the Llorente family became the protectors of something that nearly changed the world. The family owned a small farm in Basque country. Ernesto explained that he had learned his love of restoration from wandering the maze of walls that still stood on the ground floor of the old, burnt house. He showed her an engraving of it in a century-old book, a book that Agata was amazed to see was titled *The House on the Hill: The Strange Secret of Llorente Family*. It looked like a palace. She had never heard of anything like it in her family, and she was fascinated.

"The Llorentes were quite rich back then," he said. "I suppose some of us still are. They wrote this book in about 1910, at the height of Llorente power. We were a great family, for a while."

Agata remembered the old homestead. She had gone there once, when she was much younger, and recalled the long, flat farm and the rolling hills behind it. She remembered evenings spent with the family at a long, overflowing table, wine flowing and the discussion ranging from art to politics to the best time to plant potatoes. Then, suddenly, the visits to the farm stopped. No one spoke much about it, but it was clear that it was a sore spot whenever she mentioned it at home.

"Yes, you were there when you were a little girl. We don't own it anymore. The family sold it and it broke your father's heart. He loved that land. He grew up there, for a time, before your grandmother passed away."

Before they sold it, however, the Llorentes had maintained the house and kept to themselves, never selling the beef or chickens they farmed on the land or the vegetables that grew in long rows on the property. No one knew how they made their money, and the patriarch, Raul, rarely made it into the nearest city, Bilbao, sending his sons instead to trade with the villagers.

What no one knew was that the Llorentes were in charge of a massive building operation. Raul was the head of a unique and secret society of explorers who, in 1766, discovered something amazing that, in turn, changed the world forever.

The Llorentes had hired hundreds of men from surrounding villages and supplied them with raw materials to make tiles, bricks, and mortar. What the family did with these supplies was unknown—they seemed to simply collect them, and then they would disappear, gone forever. Many men told of the Llorentes' secret underground treasure rooms, but no one found anything, even when they dug through the ruins of the old house. Whatever was there was hidden to prying eyes, and wherever the supplies went, they weren't used in the Llorentes' modest home.

Where these supplies were actually going was a secret the family kept for centuries. The story was fantastical, something out of a fairy tale, but it was real. According to family lore, one member of the Llorente family, Raul's great-grandfather, José Antonio Llorente, was poaching on land near the hills. The Llorentes were farmers then, and they worked a small plot for the local count, barely making ends meet. José often went hunting on the surrounding lands. He took a flintlock rifle with him, but he was also an expert trapper and built snares to catch rabbits and, sometimes, deer.

One morning in May 1766, he set out from the farm and made his way into the woods. Tracking a boar, he ended up in a wide field near Llorente Hill, known as the *Cerro de Viento*—the Hill of Winds—for the odd winds that often rustled the tall grass and weeds that grew around it, even when the air was still.

It was near dark when he approached the hill from the south, and suddenly his horse, a skinny nag that his family had owned for five years and could barely feed, got its leg caught in a deep hole. Trapped at an odd angle, the leg broke and the horse and rider fell. Far from the village, José had to camp in the field for the night, and, after putting his horse down with his knife, he prepared for the evening.

He set up a camp near the hole the horse had fallen into, planning to move its body in the morning and sell it to the tannery. It was dark and there were wolves and wildcats in the area, so he tried to stay awake. As he sat in the quiet dark, he heard the constant sound of wind even though it was a clear, calm night.

He came to realize that the wind was coming through the hole. In the bright moonlight he looked at it closely and found it was surprisingly deep and uniform. It bored straight down into the hill and then seemed to turn and run parallel to the ground. He whistled into it and heard an echo. In his diary, he called it a "worm's hole" (*Agujero de gusano*) and was intrigued, if not obsessed by it. It was too wide to be an animal hole and too exposed. He poked at the earth around the hole with his knife, and when he found the earth was clay-rich and densely packed, he decided to return the next day to investigate. He slept the night on the hill, next to the hole, dozing and waking occasionally to see if anything—an animal or snake—ever skittered out.

As he sat, the wind continued to blow and wane, blow and wane. All he heard was the sound of whooshing air and the occasional puff of wind blowing out of the hole into the cold night. A fire he lit near the hole burned brightly all night as the slight breeze fanned the flame, picking up ashes and embers and carrying them into the night sky.

The next day José walked home—almost ten miles—and returned with a carriage and his brother, Carlos. They brought shovels and approached the hole he had covered with a broken branch. In a few hours they had increased the size of the hole—his brother kept watch on the horizon in case the owner of the land saw them—and José finally made it large enough to move through on his belly. It was about two meters deep and about a meter in diameter. It was an uncomfortable crawl, but the Llorente brothers were skinny and lithe, both lean and strong from years of hard farm work.

José wrote that he expected to find treasure or at least a shelter he could use when hunting the lands. The hole was almost invisible in the tall grass, even when they dug it wider and wider. It made no sense that it should be there, but it was.

José snaked on his belly through the hole, his hands forward, a rope tied around his legs so that his brother could pull him back out. Two meters in, he came to an open space. Pulling himself through, he asked his brother to send through a lamp and some oil. It was pitch dark, but a few moments later, José pulled a bucket holding a lamp and flint. In the meager light that came through the hole, he was able to strike the flint and light the wick. He lifted the lamp to reveal something wondrous—a wide cave seemingly carved out by nature in the bedrock of the hill.

Tall, curved walls arced up through the gloom, and somewhere water dripped in the darkness. José wrote in his diary that he felt like he was in a cathedral in the heart of the earth, a chapel to the winds. There were two tunnels at the far end of the cave, on opposite sides, both leading into darkness. Every few minutes a gust of wind blew through them, across the floor, scouring away the dust and dirt he had brought in with him from the tunnel. The room was dry and warm and smelled fresh and clean, not at all like a hole in the ground.

The floor was stone, smoothed to a slight shine, like stone walked on by countless pilgrims. He called back to his brother to follow him through.

The oddest thing, José wrote later, was that the space was bigger than the hill itself. It was gigantic, at least twenty feet tall and forty feet wide. Every footstep echoed through the darkness, and the winds blew briskly, nearly putting out his light.

Carlos pushed himself through the hole to follow his brother. He brought another lamp and some food and had spiked a rope into the ground outside with a long iron rod so that they could pull themselves back out. Carlos, too, was dumbfounded.

"It is a church. It is as big as a church," he said.

"This is no church," said José. He wasn't superstitious, but he thought for a brief moment that they had found a gate to the underworld, somewhere between worlds.

They sat there looking at the tunnel for hours, wondering where it led and what drove the wind through it. The room itself was wide, and on either side the tunnels coiled into darkness. The rounded walls of the tunnel looked like they had been carved out by a worm's passage and worn smooth by the winds that passed every minute or so. Carlos threw a handful of dust into the column of air before him and watched it be whisked away into the darkness, disappearing into the tunnel. A moment later the wind died out and all was quiet. They formulated a plan. They would tie a length of rope to the other rope they had dragged into the tunnel through the hill. This would give them a strong anchor on the outside. One of the brothers would enter the tunnel and see how deep it went.

José went out to collect another length of rope and returned to meet his brother.

"I will go," said José.

"No. I will go. You are married and with children. Tie it tight, brother."

José argued further. Carlos was younger and could still work harder. If this was a gate to hell, José was prepared to fight the devil himself. But Carlos insisted.

"It will be fine. Everything will be fine."

They waited for the wind to die down, tied the ropes tight, and Carlos stepped into the tunnel. Following the direction of the wind, he began to walk into the darkness. The rope uncoiled farther and farther, and José called in after his brother. Suddenly, the winds picked up and began to blow. The rope on the floor unspooled itself and grew taut. José called to his brother but heard no answer. The rope strained against itself and began to unravel, strands popping as the wind pulled and pulled. A moment later it snapped, and the rope disappeared into the dark, along with Carlos. José stood, aghast, as he called for his brother, his voice echoing in the endless dark.

His brother was gone, lost to the hill of winds.

CHAPTER NINE

The Llorentes

When her uncle finished the story, they sat in silence.

"That was real? All of that?" asked Agata.

"It was, and it's still real. There is still a Mytro, and there is still a way to travel, I suppose, in a way that we still don't understand," said Ernesto.

"The Llorentes decided they had to keep the secret. José swore he would find his brother, but he never could," he continued. "However, he did discover a way to use the Mytro to travel from the hill to Bilbao in a few seconds. In his grief he threw himself down the tunnel and was picked up by the wind. He wrote that he was trapped in darkness for what seemed like hours. He thought about his wife and children in Bilbao. Then, suddenly, he popped out into another dark cave. Another small hole led to the outside where he heard carriage traffic and someone mentioning the road to Bilbao. He realized he had thought of Bilbao while he was in the tunnel and now he was close to it. He would think of a destination and the winds would take him. He went back into the tunnel and thought of the hill, and he returned to it in an instant. Whatever Carlos thought when he was in the tunnel, José couldn't imagine, but he suspected all the talk of the underworld had placed Carlos in a bad place."

"José realized that the tunnel would let him carry anything he wished through the dark. A few nights later he rode the Mytro to Bilbao and opened the tunnel slightly wider. The hole was big enough for him to come and go, but when he came back the next night, there was a small, perfect door in the hole that matched the surface of the wall into which it was embedded. Something strange was happening."

"But he was a businessman. He realized he could ship things to and from the town with ease now, and he promised merchants in Bilbao that he would get them crops sooner than any of the other farmers if they paid him a bit extra. They paid him, and he whisked bushels and bushels of wheat, potatoes, and rice to and from his farm in seconds. With the extra money, he was able to buy the hill and the surrounding land and began building what amounted to a carriage run that would carry goods through the Mytro. It was a very primitive system, but it worked for years until it was upgraded to the trains you see today. He never told anyone except some of his closest business partners. The Mytro was a Llorente secret for almost a century."

"So carriages would work as well? Would anything work?"

"There's no telling. No one knows. Whatever metaphor you use, the Mytro remains a means of transport. To transport something, you usually need a vehicle," said Ernesto. "We have only scant information because much of this was destroyed by José before he died. He didn't want the Mytro to run after his death. It had taken his brother—somewhere, he supposed—and he didn't want it to take anyone else. That's why it took so long for your father and me to discover the truth."

Agata sat, stunned.

"The Mytro uses vehicles not because it has to, but because it makes it easier for us to understand it. The family even named it, calling it Mytro after the first Metro lines. Before the carriage, you were sucked in, and you ended up who knows where, somewhere far from your home. But then they added vehicles, which made it easier for humans to understand. But when you have a vehicle, you need a map," he said.

He walked over to a gray metal filing cabinet and pulled out a sheaf of papers, old ones, held together with a rusted metal staple. "This is one. It's mine, but I have a copy that I'm going to give you. The only way to survive on the Mytro—the only way—is to have the map. You choose a location and you will go there. Otherwise, you can get lost forever, moving from station to station and never getting out. That's what I believe happened to Carlos. He couldn't find his way out."

She thought of her ancestor barreling through the dark, unable to stop or even imagine where he could end up. Did he die of exposure? Thirst? Hunger? Was he still alive, somewhere in that hole?

"So that's where my father is? In the Mytro? Like Carlos?"

"I believe so, but not like Carlos. Your father is too smart for that. And I believe your mother is there too. The Llorentes were a part of a very elite group of people for many years. For most of the 19th century, they were considered the foremost experts—dare I say controllers—of the Mytro. That was until the last 20 years, when the family forgot about its duties. Something changed in the Mytro as well. People seemed to forget about it, or at least forget how to access it."

He brought something up on his computer. It was a map, digitized, with some of the lines marked in green and others marked in red.

"This is something your father and I were working on. It's a map of safe lines, although we can't even be sure what 'safe' really means on the Mytro. It seems that there are lines that just don't work right now, and the only way to avoid them is to get off at certain points.

"We've only just recently rediscovered how the Mytro works, Agata, so it is still very dangerous to go alone. We'll need to be careful. But I think the men who took your mother are on the Mytro, and that's where they took her."

He spread another map out on his desk, pointing a long, tanned finger at a spot indicating his street. The map was ragged, pieced together again and again with cellotape and glue. It was written in a cramped hand, the lines intersecting in a thicket of words that made Agata's head swim.

"This is a few blocks down from my home. Your father and I used this stop often, when we were relearning the Mytro's secrets. Your house is here," he said, sliding his finger to another dot. This map had international lines spiking off into the ocean and coming up at various places in the United States and the rest of Europe. It stopped at Manhattan on one side and St. Petersburg on the other, and it looked like the map had been ripped off at either edge.

"There's more, here?" said Agata. It was more a statement than a question.

"Yes, there is. That's what your father was trying to find. We haven't been able to transfer the safe lines from the computer to here yet. What must be done is a methodical physical study, and your father didn't want me to do it. He said it wasn't safe. Why he went ahead and did it himself with you and your mother to care for is beyond me."

"Where is he, then?"

"Somewhere here or here," said her uncle, waving a hand at the empty space at the edges of the map. "We don't know. If he had come up, we would have been able to find him—at least he could call us. But he's never surfaced. I suspect he might have found something that neither of us expected to."

"Like what?"

"Something very, very special. Something like the end of one line and the beginning of another."

A hard knock on the door stirred them from their reverie. Then the sound of glass breaking brought them both to attention.

"They've come," whispered her uncle. His face was stone as he pushed the map and a stack of notebooks into her hand. "Take these—put them away quickly."

"Who?" asked Agata, frantic.

"The men who took your mother. Go through the back window and to the stop around the corner. It looks like a wall with the number 13 painted on it. I marked it myself. Push on it and go through. Go to New York, Central Park. Remember: when you board, think only the words 'Central Park South,' in English, over and over again. I will meet you there in a little while. There is a man named Kincaid there. He may be able to help you. I've known him only briefly, and I believe we can trust him."

"Do you have a phone? How will I find him?"

"I'll find you when they are gone," said her uncle. More glass breaking. The sound of the front door opening, slowly.

"How?"

"Go! Remember: Central Park South. Be careful, please, Agata. Listen to Mr. Kincaid but keep your wits about you. You're a smart girl, the smartest I know. Your parents will be proud when they hear how you're handling yourself."

Agata jumped up and over her uncle's low drafting table and to the window. She turned the handle to open it while her uncle ran to lock his office door. She poked her head out, looked one way and then the other, and jumped down, a slight pain in her ankle warning her that she landed wrong. She turned back to see her uncle closing the window behind her.

"What will they do to you?" asked Agata. Her uncle was framed in the window, his face pale.

"Nothing. They probably want to ask questions, but I will stall them. I'll tell you when you get to New York. Remember, Agata, this is important: when you get on the train, say 'Central Park South.' Repeat it. You can think the destination, but I want you to say it to be sure."

"Central Park South," she said.

"If we are separated for long, locate the man named Kincaid. He is an archeologist. He will help you. Remember to say those words exactly. Exactly, Agata, please."

"Who is this Kincaid? How will I find him?"

"You've met him, a long time ago, when you were a little girl. I'll text you his number. When you find him, tell him your map will lead him to the Key."

The door behind her uncle flew open.

"Remember: tell him the map will lead you to the Key. Run," he said. She paused.

"Run!"

CHAPTER TEN

Run

Agata ran through her uncle's spacious and lush backyard, through tall plants and grasses. A small vegetable garden gave off a rich, hot scent of new tomatoes. She pushed through the brush and to the wall, feeling along it for the iron door that had been bolted into it years and years ago, before Agata was born. It was hard to open, she knew, but it would let her out into the street.

The door was hidden by a tall stand of creeper vine, and it took a moment for her to find it, her hands rushing through the brush to feel the hard corner of the stone jamb and the cold of the metal. She found the handle and turned it. It creaked down and began to move on its hinges, but it would give only an inch.

Behind her she heard a gunshot and began to cry.

"Go, Agata, go," yelled her uncle from inside the house.

The door still gave her trouble, but it was starting to move. She pulled harder and it opened more, groaning on its rusted hinges. Finally she had the door open wide enough to snake through, pulling it shut behind her.

She was in an alley. In front of her, splattered in spray bomb on the back wall of an old garage she had never seen open was the number 13, faded a bit from the bright sun but still clearly visible, even under a mesh of other graffiti. Someone had tried to wash off a corner but someone else—probably her uncle—had repainted it. Running to it, she pushed on the center of the number, right at the midpoint of the three. Nothing happened.

She looked both ways and pushed harder. Somehow, the wall gave way, and she was falling inward into a cushion of air. It sucked her in and then slammed the door behind her. When she turned to look at the door, she discovered that on this side it was iron, just like the one in her uncle's garden, but with no handle. She tried to push the door back open the other way, but she couldn't budge it.

She was inside the Mytro. Her father may have been here, but now he was somewhere else on the line, somewhere very far away.

She was standing in what looked like a long train station with a platform running in front of her. (East to west? North to south? She couldn't tell.) Rails ran along in both directions in front of her and disappeared into tunnels. The air in the small, close station buzzed with something like electricity. It was no more than five feet to the platform and the whole station was tiled in brown, unglazed adobe. Her skin prickled with goose bumps as a breeze lifted and began to swirl some loose leaves into the air around her feet. The leaves blew away from her and down the tunnel, into the dark.

Suddenly a train roared into the station and stopped, its wheels ticking on the steel. The doors chimed and opened.

The train was clearly waiting for her and only her, and the scent of hot oil, dust, and some sort of spice greeted her as she boarded. Perhaps this train ran through the market in Barcelona, picking up scents like a bee rushing through a puff of pollen? Immediately, the train started moving and she thought, *What now?*

The surprise at seeing the station and concern for her uncle had blanked her mind. She rustled through her recent memory, trying to recall his instructions. *New York*, she thought, and the train began speeding up, pitching her into a wicker seat.

A moment later she was in New York.

She stood in the gloom of the darkened city hall station—"City Hall" was written in gold above the door, the station dimly lit by guttering gas lamps. She watched the train roar away and then another one took its place a minute later. That one roared away.

Another train blew into the station, the door opened in front of her, and two men came through. Both wore dark masks and one held a small pistol.

Agata had only a moment to think as the hot spike of fear rolled through her and made the back of her mouth tingle and burn. She backed up as the men moved in, their eyes scanning the gloom and then coming back to her.

"You need to stand still, miss," one said in Spanish.

She froze in terror. As the two men—both wearing dark jackets and dark slacks and military boots that crunched on the tile—came toward her, the Mytro train chimed and the doors slammed shut. A blast of air from the tunnels pushed them all to the side and one of the men dropped his gun. Strangely, the doors all opened again, and Agata turned and dove back into the car. There were only a few heartbeats between her hitting the floor and the sound of the smoothly clicking doors closing behind her.

"Stop!"

The man with the gun had already recovered it and he fired. The bullet hit the window and shattered it, pouring glass onto her back. She covered her face and eyes. Another bullet splintered the window on the far side of the car. The train started to accelerate.

As she stood up, she peered back through the connecting doors at the end of the old train. The wicker seats near her were covered in glass, so she moved backwards, toward the front of the car. She heard another hoarse shout.

"Stop! Stop!"

They were on the train with her. They must have jumped onto it as the doors were closing. The men moved toward her and tried the door handle, which was locked—although Agata couldn't see how. She worried they might try to shoot the lock. As she watched them, the train rolled into the tunnel and everything went black.

Central Park South, she thought. *I need to go to Central Park South.*

And a moment later, out of the darkness, the station appeared. It was like a scene change in a movie—blackness one moment, light in the next.

She heard a swish and the doors in her car opened. She ran for the platform and then toward a door on the far wall where she found an iron handle embedded in thick wood. She pushed, pulled, pushed. Nothing. It wouldn't budge. She pounded, screamed. A shot rang out, and she heard it smash into the brick and tile next to her head. Then, just as the men were about to reach her, the handle turned down and the door opened. A second later she was outside. Safe.

Agata had been speaking for most of the train ride. She spoke quietly, her lightly accented English calm and collected. She told Turtle the whole story, and Turtle believed her. It was too wild, too convoluted to be a lie. After all, he had ridden the Mytro himself; he knew it existed. He just didn't understand the complexity.

When she finished her story, Turtle looked up.

"That's amazing," he said.

"It's crazy, yes? Insane?"

"Then what happened?"

"I left the train as quickly as I could, and you opened the door for me. It was luck. Pure luck. If they had gotten out a second earlier, well ..."

"So you said you wanted to be in New York ..."

"I thought it," said Agata.

"And you're here. But you can only go where the map takes you?"

"I think so. I said New York and it took me to that one station, City Hall?"

"Yes, City Hall. South of where we were. So when you think 'New York,' it takes you to a landmark. If you think about a certain place, it takes you there.

"So you have to know where you're going..."

"To get there, yes," she said.

Pieces of the story echoed in Turtle's head as they climbed the subway stairs, and he stood blinking in the sunlight, unsure where

to take Agata. He imagined what he'd say to his grandmother—
"This is Agata. She's staying with us. She's an exchange student"—
and how ridiculous that would sound. Maybe he could explain that
her host parents had left town on an emergency? Maybe he could
get the Kincaids to back up his story? There was no way he'd be
able to tell her the absolute truth, especially after what Agata had
gone through.

They walked along the leafy streets of Bay Ridge, past old
duplex houses made of dark brick and the kebab restaurants that
lined Fifth Avenue. Agata took it all in, wide-eyed and smiling, still
holding Turtle's hand. He prayed it wouldn't sweat and it didn't,
staying cool and dry in her grasp.

She looked at him, right into his eyes. "Thank you, Turtle."

"For what?"

"For understanding."

They came to his house, a small, thin brick home with a carefully
tended front yard and gold numbers over the old wooden door. He
rang the doorbell and then took out his key. His grandmother wasn't
home. She was at the retirement center, probably in the kitchen
cooking dinners for folks who couldn't leave their apartments.
According to the note she left, she'd be back in a few hours, and
she wrote that there was spaghetti and garlic bread in the oven, still
warm.

Agata plugged her phone in and turned it on. She turned it on
with a swipe. No messages. Agata looked down sadly and then up
at Turtle.

"Your grandmother is very kind," said Agata. "But where are
your parents?"

"My parents died when I was a baby, in a car wreck," said Turtle.
"She and my grandfather raised me and then Grandpa died three
years ago. Pneumonia."

"It's terrible to lose people," said Agata. She looked down,
almost crying. "Do you remember them?"

"I do, barely. What's wrong?"

"I don't want to lose my parents," she said.

"But your uncle said your parents weren't dead, just gone.
Probably on the Mytro, right?"

She sniffed and shrugged.

"Have you had spaghetti before? Do you like it?"

She looked up at him, and the sadness quickly left her eyes. She laughed, her high voice seeming to fill his grandmother's small, clean kitchen with sunlight.

"Of course, Turtle. I've eaten it. Thank you," she said, finally smiling.

CHAPTER ELEVEN

The Voice of the Rails

411 disembarked at the Central Park South station and assessed the damage. The men's stray bullets had hit the wooden door, and he would have to send a younger Nayzun to repair it. He brushed his long fingers over the scars, remembering the many times he had repaired damage to the Mytro, damage caused by the hands of careless men.

There were many fools who tried to control the Mytro. Some used it as their private carriage, keeping others out by force. Others hauled slaves and goods through it, defiling the stations with animal droppings and other dirt. The Mytro controlled the Mytro. Any time humans overstepped their bounds, the Mytro would react.

The last time the Mytro shut itself down was when the men in New York tried to sell tickets to ride the Mytro, creating a network of lines that would carry paying customers over the ocean for a few pennies a trip. The Mytro put a stop to that with a fire that engulfed most of the New York stations. The stations took years to rebuild—the Nayzuns never repaired stations then, only the cars and the tunnels—and, as a testament to the humans' foolishness, the Mytro had spared the old ticket booths, which now sat, their glass windows like dead eyes recounting man's folly.

Let them try it again, the Mytro had seemed to say that day. But, then again, the Mytro never spoke. It gave orders only through the rails and the rails spoke, their metal ringing out a chorus of instruction.

411 stood, quietly, in the dark station, listening to the tracks. The flickering gas lamps reduced to wisps of light since no humans were near. The child had left the station here, they told him, and then gone to the surface where she used the humans' own trains to get away. She had crossed the river, that much was certain, the rails told him, their language more picture than word, images swimming up into 411's head like figures out of a mist.

He asked for an image of the men who had fired the gun in the Mytro, and the rails brought up a picture of two men wearing black masks. They had a map so they could go anywhere. They were not as helpless as they seemed.

They are still in New York. They just left for Brooklyn, but they are waiting for something. They are waiting outside the station. They fear the station. They fear the Mytro. There are others though. They will be more important. You must watch the men, but when I see the others, they will become your priority. 411 called another train, and a moment later it came, the doors hissing open to admit him. It would be one of the few times he had ever sat inside the trains, and he relished the moment of freedom before the doors closed and whisked him away through the darkness.

CHAPTER TWELVE

The Map

Agata and Turtle sat in the kitchen, sharing dinner.

"Tell me how you found the Mytro," said Agata. Turtle began to talk about Nate and Nick, how they used the Mytro to get around and cheat in gym, and how they swore him to secrecy.

"What was their surname?" asked Agata.

"Surname?"

"Last name?" she said.

"Nick and Nate Kincaid."

"So maybe they know the Mr. Kincaid I know?"

Turtle thought for a minute.

"It's a big city, but stranger things have happened. I have their number," he said. "They gave it to me."

"Don't call yet," she said. "Let me think." Agata swallowed a bit of garlic bread.

"This is some of my father's research," she said. She wiped her hands on a napkin, pulled a small black notebook out of her backpack, and began thumbing through the pages. Turtle could see that they were covered with dense, tiny handwriting, drawings, and diagrams.

Mytro seems to have a mind of its own, she read, translating from Spanish. *During World War II it opened itself to certain groups and individuals, allowing them to discover it in times of need. But the Mytro is not always ... beneficial? Whatever controls it is not kind and is not patient. It is very dangerous, and it will put people in places they may not want to be in order to promote its own unknowable interests.*

"What does that mean?"

"That it's not just a train line, I guess," said Agata.

Turtle nodded, pretending to understand. It certainly *seemed* smart, letting him in when it did then bringing Agata into his life.

"So maybe it meant to connect you with Nick and Nate and found me instead," said Turtle.

"Perhaps, or maybe it has other plans," she said.

Turtle shivered a bit at the thought. Everything made sense, but it was light years away from anything he had ever imagined. If someone had told him there was a system of tunnels hidden all these years, hidden in plain sight, controlled by something that could think ... if he hadn't been in the tunnels himself, he wouldn't have believed it. And now this?

"How can it exist? How can no one find it?"

"My father wrote more," she said. She flipped a few more pages. *It's always and forever hidden. The tunnels aren't there, but when they are, they repair themselves when damaged and hide themselves when threatened.*

World War II: The Germans were near to finding a station in Dresden. The firebombs had destroyed one of the hiding places, and one of the Mytro doors was open and exposed. As the Germans began pounding on the door, it splintered and fell away. Behind it was a stone wall, completely bare. The Mytro had prevented them from finding the door, but a man, a man who knew about the Mytro, had watched what happened from a nearby building, and so he knew the secret was still safe. When he went back after the war, he put up another door and suddenly, just like magic, the station was back.

"Just like magic, huh? So who built the trains? They weren't always there? The conductors? Does anyone know?"

Agata thumbed through the pages.

"Nay-zuns?" she read.

"What?"

"That's what my dad wrote: Nayzuns." She spelled it. *The Nayzuns repair the tunnels.*

"But those trains. Those are old trains, and people built them. Those aren't space vehicles or anything."

She checked further. Nothing. She shook her head.

"It doesn't say. I know as much as you know." She grinned slyly. It was nice to see her smile.

"So where do we go now?"

"Maybe I'll go back to Barcelona, see if my dad is back," she said. "Let's look at the map."

She pulled a thick sheaf of papers out of her bag and began spreading them out. They were once part of one big sheet of paper, but they ripped at the creases, turning it into more of a pamphlet. Once they spread it out on the counter, Turtle was able to understand the scale of the Mytro. Almost every inch of the map was covered with tiny, cramped handwriting. Lines crisscrossed the globe, from Russia to China to France to America. The U.S. map spanned several dozen pages with multiple lines marked in different colors. Some of the stations were crossed out while others were nameless—just question marks in the middle of a desert or a forest. Some of them were checked off in red pencil. Her father, ever the teacher, used red pencil. He had been there, in those stations. Her father was riding each train and taking each stop just to see where it let him off. That's why it seemed like he was always missing.

"Can I make a copy of this?" asked Turtle.

"Sure," said Agata. They moved over to the computer room on the first floor where his grandmother had her scanner. Turtle fed the map into the scanner and then printed each page, collecting the copies into a pile. It took nearly twenty minutes to scan all the pages, and Turtle worried the brittle pages would crumble in the process.

"So when your dad was gone, he was on the Mytro, right?"

"I think so," she said. "He definitely wasn't upstairs."

"OK, so here's the plan: we have to get you back to Barcelona, and we have to find your parents. I can come with you for a little while, until my grandma comes back. Then I can use this map to get home. Let's call Nick and Nate. Maybe they can help us."

"Thank you, Turtle," said Agata as the paper spooled from the buzzing printer. "It's nice to have a friend."

CHAPTER THIRTEEN

Chase

411 disembarked in Brooklyn. He sensed the two men outside the door to the Prospect Park Station, waiting for a signal of some sort. They were tense. 411 and his kind could not feel emotion, but they could see it in humans. Fear was blue, and these men were pulsing a rich cerulean, even through the thick stone walls. Somewhere down the line, he could sense the children and the man who wanted to intercept them. He knew they were important to whatever the Mytro was planning. The girl in particular. She wore something that flashed like a phosphor flare through the tunnels. Every Nayzun could see it, even from the Hangar. It was like watching a torch on a dark plain, bobbing in the distance.

411 lived on the tangents, the places where the Mytro just barely kissed the edge of the earth. The Key was moving between those tangents, from the bright lines of the Mytro into the dirt and dust of the human world. Unlike the humans who needed their feet or vehicles to move from one spot to the next, the Nayzuns moved behind the scenes wherever they wished. They rode the Mytro occasionally, but they didn't have to. They could just ride the lines between stations.

Now 411 moved from one tangent to the next, coming closer to the men on the train.

411 remembered all the safeguards put into place to keep evil men from using the Mytro for evil things. Clearly these safeguards were failing, one by one, as the humans began to truly understand

the Mytro and its power. The shooting was just the beginning. They felt at ease enough here now to bring their own odd customs to the rails.

The children and the men are on a collision course. Stop them, whined the rails. 411 took another turn and began to trail them, the rails singing his footsteps like a hollow prayer.

CHAPTER FOURTEEN

The Phone Call

Turtle dialed Nick and Nate's number with the prestigious 212 area code—most Brooklyn numbers, like Turtle's, started in 718.

On the fourth ring an older man picked up. Nick and Nate's parents were divorced, and their father lived in Europe and never came to New York. Turtle had no idea what to do.

"Hello?" said the voice.

"Hello, is Nick or Nate there?" he asked.

"Who is this?"

Turtle paused. He looked at Agata, his eyes wide, and thought about the men chasing her and her parents.

"Who is this?" the gruff voice repeated and Turtle hung up. His heart was racing. Did the Kincaids have a way of calling him back? Did they know his number?

They sat there quietly as Turtle checked the number again. He reached for the phone, and suddenly it buzzed in his hand, ringing loudly in the quiet kitchen. He nearly dropped it.

Turtle looked at Agata then at the phone. "Answer?" he asked.

She nodded, once.

"Hello? Hello?" The gruff voice was there, but it seemed kinder now, a bit worried. "Is this Nick's friend Lizard?" said the voice. "Are you safe?"

"Turtle. They call me Turtle. We're safe, yes. Who is this?"

"I'm Tom Kincaid, Nick's uncle. He told me you'd call. You're in danger. Is the girl with you?"

"How do you know—"

"I know her family. Our research overlapped. I'm coming to get you. Where do you live?"

Turtle covered the phone.

"He wants to know where we are," he said.

"Tell him, please," said Agata.

Pressing the speaker button on the phone, Turtle rattled off his address, his voice filling the kitchen.

"Don't leave the house. I'm in a silver Jeep with "Advanced Urban Archeology" written on the side. Don't get into any other car."

"How long will it take you?"

"If I catch the right train maybe five minutes. I'll see you shortly. Please trust me. The girl is in great danger. I was on the same mission as her father and I knew him well. She might remember me. I met her in Barcelona when she was very little. Can I speak to her?"

Turtle looked at her again. She nodded.

"*Hola, Señor* Kincaid," she said. Mr. Kincaid began to speak to her in Spanish, and they went back and forth for a few minutes. "*Si, si. Yo recuerdo,*" she said, smiling. "I remember him," she said. "He was at one of my uncle's parties."

"You kids are doing the right thing," said Mr. Kincaid. "I'll see you both in a little bit."

"Thank you, Mr. Kincaid," said Agata.

"Agata, do you have any of your father's things?"

"Yes, some of them."

Mr. Kincaid was quiet.

"I'll be right over. Don't open the door until I get there."

They went to the front window to watch the street. Turtle wondered at what Mr. Kincaid had said—"if I catch the right train"—how could he get here in five minutes on a train ... especially if he was driving?

Mr. Kincaid's silver Jeep pulled up 13 minutes later. The top was down, and Mr. Kincaid was wearing big sunglasses, khaki pants, and a black T-shirt. He looked like Nick and Nate—tall, lanky, darker blonde hair and a weather-beaten face that showed he lived or worked outdoors. The Jeep had "Advanced Urban Archeology" written on the side, with two crossed shovels over a pile of bricks.

He stopped the car in front of Turtle's house and walked up to the front door. He rang curtly, tapping the bell quickly twice in succession. They watched him from the front window and then, after Agata nodded again, Turtle opened the door.

Mr. Kincaid took off his sunglasses. He had dark green eyes—the same as Nick and Nate's. He smiled when he saw Agata and she ran to him, her arms open. He hugged her tightly and then let go.

"I'll bet you never expected any of this when you woke up this morning, eh?"

"None of this," said Agata.

"You can stay here, Paul. Thank you for helping Agata."

Turtle looked at the girl and then up at Mr. Kincaid. He seemed trustworthy, but still nothing made any sense.

"Maybe I should go with you," said Turtle. "To help?"

"You can, but it could be dangerous. There's no reason to bring you further into this."

"Maybe not, but I'd feel better. After all, she's kind of my responsibility. She found me in the park, and I'd like to make sure she's safe."

Mr. Kincaid raised one eyebrow quizzically, and Agata laughed. "I remember you being able to do that," she said. "From when I was a girl. He could also blow smoke rings."

"I don't smoke anymore, but if I did, I'd blow some for you," said Mr. Kincaid. Then he looked at Turtle.

"If you want to come, that's fine, but understand that things are getting very complex very fast and that the Mytro is a very weird place," he said. "At the very least, I promised Nick and Nate I'd show you a bit of the system."

Turtle looked down at his shoes and then up and Agata and Mr. Kincaid. Agata was finally beaming. "What's going on, Mr. Kincaid? Can you tell us?"

"I can tell you what I know. We need to leave though."

"I have to tell my grandma. She'll worry."

Turtle ran back to the kitchen and found a clean notepad.

"Studying at the library," he wrote in big block letters. "Be back at eight o'clock. Love, Paul."

He hoped she'd forgive the little white lie.

66

"OK," he said, returning to the front door with his keys. He carried two jackets, one for himself, a black one, and one for Agata. "I brought these in case it gets cold. I'm ready to go."

"Let's head out then, Paul."

"You can call him Turtle," said Agata and Turtle blushed.

"Turtle, eh? Slow and steady. Turtle it is. Let's go."

CHAPTER FIFTEEN

The Theatergoers

They piled into Mr. Kincaid's Jeep. It was immaculate inside, but there were two heavy marble statues on the backseat and something that looked like a wooden box wrapped in bubble wrap. Turtle sat in back next to the statues while Agata sat in front.

"Watch out for that junk back there," said Mr. Kincaid. "I buy and sell urban antiques. Those are two fireplace carvings from an old house in Greenwich Village. Lions. You don't see those anymore."

Turtle saw a snarling snout peeking out from under the plastic. The lion also looked like it was missing an ear.

"But you research the Mytro?" asked Turtle.

"I do. Agata's father and I were part of a group of researchers. You haven't heard much about that, right, Agata?" asked Mr. Kincaid.

"Nothing at all. He never talked about his work."

"There's not much to tell, but we're quite close to making some very important discoveries—or, more precisely, your father was very close when all of this happened."

He started the Jeep and drove down Turtle's street toward the subway station. For a moment, Turtle was sure they would stop by the station Turtle used to get to school, but then he remembered the Mytro.

They kept driving, turning left onto a small side street less than a mile from Turtle's house. It was an alley behind a movie theatre that he visited nearly every time a new film came out. He loved sitting alone in the dark, listening to the subway rumble underneath.

Now, however, they were heading toward the back.

"As far as I can tell, a group of men were working on the same research that your father and I were working on. They didn't get as far as your father, and they believe he has found something very important to their cause. Whether that's true or not remains to be seen.

"Your uncle Ernesto told me your father had disappeared in the Mytro. That means a few possible things happened: he's lost, which is unlikely, or he's hiding. The only way to find him is to use a set of tools he was researching. He has one copy, I suspect, and there is another one hidden somewhere.

"I believe they've taken your mother somewhere in the Mytro and they were coming for you, to bargain with your family. But if he's well and truly lost, then all their efforts may be hopeless. There's only one way to find out though: to find the things he was looking for and to use them to take control of the Mytro."

"Take control?" asked Turtle. "How?"

"You're going to have to trust me," said Mr. Kincaid. "Agata, your mother and father are inside the Mytro—I don't know where—and we can find them with the right tools. Maps to those tools are in your father's study—I'm sure of it—but we have to find them in order to set your parents free. Do you understand?"

Agata nodded.

He rolled the Jeep farther up the alley and turned on the lights. They were facing a dark gate made of heavy iron slathered in chipped black paint. There was a spot of graffiti in the upper right corner, a spray-painted number 13 in bright blaze orange, something you'd think was a gang symbol.

"My uncle sprayed that same sign on his station," said Agata.

"That's right. It's a signal. You mark stations with a 13. It's a prime number, it's unlucky-looking enough to think maybe kids wrote it, and the 3, sideways, is supposed to look like an M. It's sort of a secret symbol of the Mytratti, the people who study the Mytro."

Mr. Kincaid put the car into park, the engine still running, and got out. He opened the gate, got back in, drove the car through the gate, and then closed it behind him, the hinges screeching loudly enough that Turtle was sure someone would notice. He pulled up to what looked like a blank, brick wall and slowly edged the car forward, inch by meticulous inch, giving it a little gas and then letting go. The front bumper touched the brick, and the wall started to move and fold up on itself on invisible hinges like a garage door. The bricks, which looked heavy, then tipped up enough to let the Jeep through and then slowly fell back down, grinding into place with a sound of gravel on gravel. Turtle turned around to watch the wall fall back into place, but by the time he craned his neck enough to see, the wall had already closed with a thump.

The Jeep's front lights shot bright beams into the Mytro station. In the harsh halogen, the Mytro looked much more real, much less like something out of a museum. Wisps of dust floated in the beams and there was dirt in between the tiles, grime that seemed pressed into the cracks by whatever forces propelled the trains along the tracks and into the dark.

There was a crack in the crazed green wall tile, and there was a spot on the wall where one had fallen off. Behind the tile—as far as Turtle could tell—was packed dirt. It looked darker than normal dirt, and smooth, and none of it had fallen out, suggesting that it was packed tightly into the space behind the wall.

This Mytro platform was marked "Bay Ridge Fifth Avenue Theatre." A pair of masks, comedy and tragedy, were arrayed over the main door. The larger door they came through was now nowhere to be seen. All that remained was a small, human-sized door, made of wood and bands of iron with a simple knob that shone as if it had just been polished. Turtle looked up and down the wall to see how the door had grown so large, but there was no evidence of it ever having moved. Even the dust at the edge of the floor was undisturbed except where the Jeep's tire tracks ground it away now and, Turtle assumed, when Mr. Kincaid drove through to get them.

"So we could bring anything in here?" asked Turtle.

"A truck, probably, yes. Anything bigger and I doubt it would fit. We also got lucky with that door. When I heard the gate screech like that, I was sure we'd be spotted."

"What would happen then?" asked Agata.

"The problem with the Mytro is that if it thinks it's been seen, it will shut the door faster than you can blink," said Mr. Kincaid. "I've seen people get knocked out of the way with a gust of wind and sometimes the Mytro just won't open."

Turtle gulped as he imagined the door slamming shut on them as they rolled through.

"They built this one behind a theater. They actually used to use it to transport heavy scenery from Broadway out to this area," said Mr. Kincaid, pointing to the masks. "It's one of the few Mytro stations that was used by more than just experts for a long time. The owners of this theater knew all about it, and they had a side business, during Prohibition, running whiskey from the pier out here over to Manhattan."

"So people used these tunnels? Regularly?" asked Turtle.

"Absolutely, probably a hundred years ago. Then something happened that stopped all that. That's one of the things we were researching. We're trying to figure out what happened."

The wind suddenly picked up. A train was coming. Turtle took a deep breath and smelled the polished, dusty closeness of the small station, smaller than the ones Turtle had seen so far. It looked like an afterthought, the way some subway stations looked lonely in the outskirts of the Bronx and Queens.

This station was a little less ornate than the Central Park station. A wide platform was made of red brick and there were large, plain letters above the track bed with arrows pointing to Staten Island to the south and Green-Wood to the north. Green-Wood was the cemetery that took up most of the adjoining neighborhood, so it must have been another stop on this particular line.

Mr. Kincaid pointed toward the signs. "They put up those signs to make people feel comfortable, but in fact, the Mytro is nonlinear. There are no 'lines,'" he said.

"Not to be rude, Mr. Kincaid, but where are we going? And how are we getting there by Jeep?" asked Turtle.

"The Mytro adapts. That's what Agata's father was studying, and that's what I studied, for a while. The way it's adapting now is to protect itself from an outside enemy. That enemy is after the Mytro and they're trying to control it. That's what Agata's father and mother ran afoul of."

"And that's who was after me?" asked Agata.

"They're on the Mytro already?" Mr. Kincaid asked.

"There were men—two of them—with guns. I think they were trying to grab me in Barcelona. They shot at my uncle. I need to know if he's OK."

"This is all pointing to one thing, Agata. Did your uncle tell you about the Conductor's Key?"

"No," she said.

Suddenly, out of the dark, came the Mytro. It consisted of three cars, two passenger cars on the front and the back and a large, flatbed carrier made of filigreed iron in the middle, its bed made of roughly hewn wood. A wisp of straw peeked out from between two edge boards and fluttered into the air as the train approached the station.

"Then hang on. We're going somewhere they can't find us to think this whole thing out."

"Where?" asked Turtle.

"You're going to love this, Turtle."

The carrier came up just to the edge of the platform, which meant the entire car was far lower than the passenger cars flanking it. Mr. Kincaid maneuvered the Jeep alongside the flatbed and then onto it, parking it and pulling the handbrake for safety. Suddenly, the Mytro began to move, rattling into the darkness again, which soon overtook them. Sparks began to shoot up from the wheels as they picked up speed, and the Mytro veered to the left wildly, shaking back and forth for a moment and then righting itself and continuing on into the darkness.

"Where are we going?" yelled Agata over the screaming wind, her words ripped from her mouth.

"To Barcelona," yelled Mr. Kincaid.

The train roared on through the tunnel, and Turtle tried to count how long they were in the dark. He made it to 60 before the silence hit, a wall of total silence and space that seemed to be crystalline, the lights of the front car refracting into the darkness. Wherever they were, Turtle couldn't count anymore.

CHAPTER SIXTEEN

Barcelona

The sudden stop took Turtle's breath away. This trip had been longer than the quick one he took in Central Park, that was sure, and the air here felt different. They were in a dark, large room, and the gloom through the Jeep's windows was almost as deep as the darkness in the tunnel. Mr. Kincaid reversed his previous maneuver, turned the wheels and drove over the edge of the carrier onto the platform. He parked and turned off the engine.

"This is one of the few stations in Barcelona big enough for the car," he said. "Plus, they have great food upstairs."

They were in a station that looked less like the terminals they visited in New York and more like an unused cellar with a low, vaulted ceiling and a small door at the far end. The station smelled like mold and something fruity—rotten grapes, maybe—and now, thanks to the fading Jeep exhaust, motor oil and gasoline.

"This is an old wine cellar. It's one of the few Mytro stations that used to be used for something else," said Mr. Kincaid. The sign above the door, carved into dark, lacquered wood, read *Barcelona La Rambla*. "It's owned by a family that has done business here for two centuries."

"Why are we here?" asked Agata.

"We're home, your home. Barcelona. We're going to leave the car and walk," said Mr. Kincaid as he turned the handle and pulled open the door.

They were in a dark storeroom lined with boxes and bottles. A rack of wine gently rattled as the wind from the Mytro slammed the door shut behind them. Turtle ran his hand along the boxes of produce, marveling that everything was in Spanish. A box of strange white things turned out to be flattened fish crusted in salt. Potatoes in a big bin had started to grow stalks from their pinpoint eyes, the white tendrils creeping out of the crate and down to the floor like searching fingers.

The place smelled like a kitchen but with something a bit rotten underneath, as if the cooks hadn't cleaned out the garbage cans.

"Is this a good restaurant?" asked Turtle warily as he fingered the salted fish, his face screwing up into a grimace.

"Definitely depends on what you like," admitted Mr. Kincaid.

They walked to the end of the storeroom to a set of stone stairs leading up to a plain, brown wooden door. As they took to the stairs, the floor above creaked slightly, and the voices of the cooks seemed hushed, as if they had heard them come in and were now listening for their footsteps. Mr. Kincaid took the lead and opened the door, which led into a small, cramped kitchen. A wild-haired man wearing a chef's coat was chopping boiled eggs and smiled when he saw Mr. Kincaid. A pile of dirty dishes soaking in murky gray water in a sink near the door gave off the scent of vinegar, and a small man in a white T-shirt and white chef's pants was scrubbing pots and pans with a dirty rag. The chef nodded to the dishwasher who plopped the rag into the sink and went out a back door, shutting it behind him.

"Ah, Tom. So nice to see you!" said the chef. He wiped his hand on his apron and offered it to Mr. Kincaid.

"Julio, a pleasure. It's been too long. This is Agata and Paul. Agata is Ernesto's niece."

The chef's face paled. He looked at the girl then at Mr. Kincaid.

"Oh yes. Oh yes. I heard the news. Something very bad is happening on the Mytro. It's changing. Agata, I am pleased to finally meet you. We lived so close but we never met, I suppose. I was a friend of your father's. I admire his work. I feel sadness I was never was able to come to your home to meet you or your mother."

The cook turned to Mr. Kincaid.

"Do we know anything new?" he asked.

"No, but we're in Barcelona to find out what we can. The Mytro

74

is not acting normally.

"The Mytro is doing strange things, this is true. I've told my sons not to ride it anymore. They never listen to me, but maybe they will to you."

The chef scraped the eggs into a small bowl, covered them with a dash of oil, and then grabbed some paprika and dusted the white eggs bright red. Finally, he brushed his hands off and motioned toward the kitchen door, past a rack of plates and glasses that shone brightly in the fluorescents. "Bravo," he said. "Tom, maybe the children could have a table and perhaps eat some *paella*? You and I will talk?"

"That might be a good idea."

Julio led the two out of the kitchen into the restaurant, which was dark and cozy and shaped much like the wine cellar in the basement. Tables lined the walls and smoked tan tiles ran the length of the room. A short waiter with Julio's red hair sat them down at a table, and Julio told them to wait, smiling wanly at Agata as he left.

"What does the chef want to talk to Mr. Kincaid about?" asked Turtle in a whisper.

"I don't know, but it sounded serious," said Agata.

"I'm going to go and listen. I'll say I'm looking for the bathroom."

"No, sit."

"It's about your parents, Agata. It's important."

Turtle stood up and walked toward the back of the restaurant. The red-haired waiter, probably Chef Julio's son, glowered at him.

"Bathroom?" he asked, then, remembering his Spanish, he repeated, "*Baño?*" The waiter stuck a thumb out at a door nearby, partially blocked by a serving station covered with dirty dishes. Turtle elbowed it out of the way and fumbled a while with the handle.

Inside, he could hear what was happening in the kitchen although the sound was muffled. Above him was a heating grate embedded in the brick wall. He put the toilet seat lid down and climbed up, his ear close to the grate. Their voices became clearer.

"This girl does not know?" he heard Julio say.

"She doesn't. It got out of hand, clearly. This is not how it was supposed to work," said Mr. Kincaid. "We'll have the Key and then we'll be able to go for her parents."

75

"*If* you find the Key …," said Julio.

"It's here, Julio, she has half of it."

Julio gasped.

"So long we've waited. So long," the cook whispered.

Turtle stood there for a moment, listening to the sound of his heartbeat in his ears, then hopped down, flushed the toilet, and washed his hands. He came out of the bathroom just as Chef Julio was bringing out a steaming caldron of what Turtle thought looked like orange rice. "My friends, a celebration in honor of our guests. The best *paella* in all of Barcelona!"

CHAPTER SEVENTEEN

The Keys

Turtle had come back from the bathroom and sat down, his face ashen. He wanted to tell Agata what he had heard, but Mr. Kincaid had followed Julio into the main dining room. He began spooning the paella onto their plates, which Turtle found to be very good, if a little weird with huge shrimp, their heads and tails still attached. The food and the strangeness of it were almost enough to make him feel less queasy about Mr. Kincaid.

The only sound was Mr. Kincaid thumbing furiously through a notebook in front of him as they ate. He was scanning page after page of cramped writing and drawings. Turtle recognized some diagrams of the Mytro, but he also saw some strange objects shaped like hooks and half-moons.

He came to a section scribbled over in dark pen with plenty of crossed-out areas. There were drawings of skeleton keys and a tracing of something that looked like a jagged coin.

"Your father was looking for the Conductor's Key. There are two parts. The first half looks like this." He lifted the book to show them. "Have you seen it?"

On the page was a strange circular object with a part cut out at a jagged angle. Agata was wearing it around her neck, and she tensed when she saw it. Sitting across from her, Turtle shook his head slightly, just an infinitesimal movement he hoped she'd pick up. Their eyes met for a moment, and Turtle hoped she understood: *Don't say anything*, he screamed in his head.

"No, never," she said. "Dad never told us what he was working on. Maybe it's at the house?"

"Indeed. There are actually two Keys," said Mr. Kincaid. "As far as we've been able to tell, two have to be used simultaneously. This is called the Conductor's Key. It's much more complex," said Mr. Kincaid, pointing at a drawing of a long skeleton key with a huge fob at one end. It seemed to be covered with dials and tiny switches. Then he pointed to the other shape, the part Agata wore.

"This is the Railman's Key. Together, they seem to be able to control the Mytro. Your father had been working to find the Conductor's Key, and we think he already found the Railman's Key."

"So where are they?" asked Turtle.

"He was very conscientious, so I suspect he wrote everything down. We need his notes," said Mr. Kincaid. "And I think they're in his office. We need to check. Can you take us to your home?"

Agata sat still for a moment.

"I'm scared," she said. "But we should go."

"Don't be scared," said Mr. Kincaid. "I'll be with you."

That, thought Turtle, is what they should be afraid of.

CHAPTER EIGHTEEN

La Rambla

The three left the restaurant in the dark of night. Barcelona was six hours ahead of New York, so the moon was already full and near the horizon. The dislocation—from afternoon to late evening made Turtle's head spin.

Turtle was glad he brought a jacket. A chill, wet air had settled over the city, and light fog flitted between the throngs of people on La Rambla, a wide boulevard flanked on either side by smaller roads. They walked toward Agata's house, Mr. Kincaid in the lead. Turtle pulled Agata back to him.

"Mr. Kincaid," he said, loudly enough, he thought, to be heard over the din. However, Mr. Kincaid kept walking; he couldn't hear them. Turtle turned to Agata.

"I don't know if we can trust Mr. Kincaid. I overheard him talking in the kitchen. He knows you have the coin. I have no idea what's going on. Just act normal."

Mr. Kincaid turned around to look at them.

"You guys look tired," he said as they negotiated the crowds on La Rambla. They passed a newsstand and then ended up in an area with stalls selling parakeets and finches, their songs clashing wildly with the car horns in the road and the rapid-fire Spanish.

"We're fine," said Turtle. "At least I am."

"I'm fine, too," said Agata.

Turtle read the neon signs they passed: *Tapas, Cigarillos, Pan*. It was all wildly foreign to him, and he wished he had a camera to take a picture for his grandmother. His grandmother! She would be waiting for him, he was an ocean away from her, time was ticking away, and whatever they were doing here involved grown men with guns. He wanted desperately to go home.

Turtle looked over at Agata. She was alone. Her parents were gone, she had no one to protect her, and clearly Mr. Kincaid was up to something. As they walked along La Rambla, he decided he would see this to its end with her.

Even so, Turtle thought for a moment about bolting—grabbing Agata's hand and running into the crowd. Mr. Kincaid knew how to use the Mytro, and he probably had people all around the city watching for him. A vision of the net they had fallen into was forming in his mind, although he was barely able to believe that Mr. Kincaid could be a danger to him or Agata.

Agata grabbed his hand and squeezed it.

A turn between two stalls selling rich, pungent roses brought them to Agata's street. They stopped at her front door where a small metal sign above the bell read *Llorente*.

Agata looked at Turtle, then at Mr. Kincaid.

"You're going to have to trust me," said Mr. Kincaid. "We're going to find them, Agata. I promise."

She pulled her key out of her stuffed backpack and turned it in the lock. The door swung slowly open. After an afternoon of sudden, rushing winds coming from behind wooden doors, the silence behind this one was a welcome relief.

"Up the stairs, guys. Let's figure this out," said Mr. Kincaid.

CHAPTER NINETEEN

Protection

The rails sang to the Nayzun. The Mytro had a message.
The men are trying their tricks again.
A pause. The music vibrated in the air.
Is that all? the Nayzun asked. *Is there more?*
Yes, there is more, said the rails, a voice like the clatter of iron wheels through a dark tunnel, a sound that clacked and clacked, Dopplering off into the darkness. *The two children. Protect them. The girl's parents have been taken by those who wish to play their tricks. They must be kept safe, all of them.*
Humans? Keep the humans safe?
These four are important. The mother and the daughter, the father of the girl, and the boy.

411 thought about the last time he had considered humans to be important, humans who move above, rustling through the grass like rabbits. The Nayzuns did not maintain the tracks for the humans. They maintained the tracks because that was their warrant.

Long ago, before 411 was born, there were questions asked about the humans. Were they free? Why did they not toil like the Nayzuns? Why were their limited desires met by the Mytro at the cost of Nayzun toil? The Mytro quickly quashed these questions with violence. There was a Great Cleansing and many Nayzuns were destroyed.

But more recently, 411 had been thinking about the humans.

What part did they all play in this skein of interconnected tracks? Were the humans the riders? Why were the Nayzuns relegated to working in the dark while the humans walked around in the light?

Those sorts of questions could bring great danger to 411 and his people. Although 411 didn't feel anything the humans would call affection for his fellow workers, he knew that, in the end, every life was important.

The Nayzun considered his next steps. The rails had told him where the girl was and where the men were. He would have to protect the children in the Mytro. It was a dark, strange place without a map, and, though the girl had many tools with her, they might not be enough.

A thought went through 411's mind, a wisp of an idea. Maybe the humans were there to save the Nayzun? Eyes that had not seen white could never see black, the old Nayzun saying went. 411 couldn't imagine freedom.

He was given his orders. He would complete them. The children would be protected as long as they were in the Mytro.

Go. Do not fail, said the rails. Failure, 411 knew, was not an option.

CHAPTER TWENTY

The Leaning Door

The trio climbed two flights of stairs with Agata leading the way, past the locked doors of the other two flats in the building, and finally came to the Llorente apartment. She unlocked the door with another big key and led the others into a darkened foyer lined with shoes and coats.

The apartment was cold, and the stillness in the air unnerved Turtle. Through the door it looked like the apartment was in disarray, but it was dark and they couldn't see much. Then Agata flicked on some lights and the extent of the damage became clear.

Many of the cabinets had been ransacked, items strewn everywhere. Some of the coats that clotted the front hall had been stomped on, and the television was overturned. Pictures had been taken down from the walls, the glass broken to check behind the images. There was a whiff of vanilla and a deeper scent that reminded Turtle of the orange paella.

"Geez," said Turtle.

"They must have done this after I left," said Agata, choking back tears. Turtle led her past the living room and into the dining room then into a little hall that led to the kitchen. Here there was less damage, but it was still a mess.

"The study is up here," she said, pointing at a wrought-iron spiral staircase. She turned on a light and began climbing, her footsteps clanging on the steps.

When they reached the top, all three of them stopped. It looked like the room had exploded. Agata began to cry, a tear rolling down her left cheek to her chin.

Books and papers lay scattered on the floor, and many of the filing cabinets had been gutted, their contents pulled out and crushed on the desk and chairs. Whoever had ransacked the place threw books from the bookshelf, leaving their spines shattered. A computer monitor lay facedown on the floor surrounded by a halo of broken glass. A huge stack of papers lay in a rainbow from the stairs down to the far end of the attic.

Agata moaned, long and softly. She turned to face Turtle and buried her face in his shoulder. "Where is he?" she asked. "Where's my father?"

Turtle looked around. The room looked like the attic of a train buff. There were pictures of old subway trains, a few printed schedules, and a whole wall covered in pinned-up train track maps from the 1970s, their colors faded and the paper turning yellow with age.

On one wall, in a huge, ornate frame, was an etching of a statue of an angel falling from the sky. Underneath it Turtle read *Parque Del Buen Retiro, Madrid.* In bold black letters was the word *Lucifer.* The devil.

Turtle shuddered and cast his gaze on the rest of the room. Certain things were immediately apparent when you knew what to look for. What train had a stop in the middle of the Pacific Ocean, as one large map was marked? Why would a normal subway stop five times in the middle of Central Park, in Manhattan, where inked train lines crisscrossed the city like a spider's web? As Turtle looked more closely, none of the trains represented on the wall existed in real life. There were drawings of Mytro passenger and carrier cars featuring hand-drawn annotations showing various parts of the control panel and wheel structure. Maps covered every inch of exposed wall, carefully outlining the various stops. Many of these drawings and maps had been torn down, wisps of paper still hanging from metal thumbtacks pushed into the plaster and crumpled in a pile near the edges of the room. Someone had punched a hole in the wall, as if looking for something hidden behind it.

Turtle's foot brushed what looked like a huge, squashed bug made of electronics: someone had stepped on a computer mouse, splaying it open. The force and anger that it must have taken to squash it like that was frightening.

Next to the desk was a plain wooden door leaning up against the wall. It was still in its frame and was reinforced with light wooden two-by-fours around the edge. The door was slightly damaged—there were scratches along the surface, and the green brass handle was slashed a few times with something sharp and hard, the corroded metal cut away to expose the brighter metal underneath. Someone had written a small numeral 13 on the wood in black marker.

Mr. Kincaid walked over to the door and tapped it once, lifting it away from the wall and then putting it back. He smiled broadly.

"Now this is a fascinating creation. It's a byproduct of the Conductor's Key. Clearly your father knew what he was doing," he said. "It takes a person with a special understanding of the Mytro to use this. It was one of the best kept secrets of the Blitz."

There was a hasp on the door, roughly screwed into the worn wood, and an open padlock hung from it. Mr. Kincaid pulled off the padlock and put it into his pocket. Then he reached out to turn the handle and, with a click, opened the door.

It looked like a magician's trick: through the door was a station—ever so gently slanted because of the angle of the door to the wall. It was complete and quite small, similar in size to the wine cellar they had used to enter the restaurant. As Mr. Kincaid held open the door, a gust of wind threatened to shut it again as the Mytro stormed down the tracks.

The sight of the Mytro through this odd door took Turtle's breath away. It was easy to imagine dragons and castles and ancient wizards, but to see magic in real life—or what Turtle imagined was magic—was something else entirely.

A moment later the train doors closed and the train was off again. The chime echoed in the attic. Mr. Kincaid closed the door before the next train roared through.

"That's amazing," muttered Turtle.

"It really is," said Agata. "I had no idea he had this. Now I know what he was doing. Some nights I'd hear that bell, that chime."

"There were a few of these made around the world, but I thought all of them had been destroyed. Your father was very good at understanding and harnessing the technology that controlled the Mytro. Very, very good. You can be proud, Agata," said Mr. Kincaid.

Looking at the door made Turtle queasy. He realized that the Mytro was nowhere, that the Mytro didn't exist in any way he could easily understand. It was a space that could hold multitudes but, in the end, wasn't really there. Mr. Kincaid placed the lock back into the hasp, unlocked.

"Now we need to find your father's Map. Every Mytro scholar has their own, but I'm sure your father's is much more interesting. Maybe there's a clue on there," said Mr. Kincaid.

"Who did all this damage?" asked Turtle as he picked up the fallen pages and tried to put them back into order.

"Enemies," said Mr. Kincaid.

"My father had no enemies. He was a scientist," said Agata angrily.

"Sadly, that isn't true. This is a strange world. Some people who studied the Mytro, the Mytratti, thought your father was a rebel. They asked him for his work, tried to buy it, tried to coerce him with threats. He didn't want to share his work, and he was so far advanced that it was an absolute shame. There are many who, like him, had dedicated their lives to the Mytro. They were angry he wouldn't share his knowledge."

"Maybe he had good reason," said Agata.

"Maybe," said Mr. Kincaid.

CHAPTER TWENTY-ONE

Ascent

411 began his slow ascent. He had to arrive before the children left Barcelona. He had to protect them. The men who had caused so much trouble were the least of his concern now. The Mytro would stop *them*.

He moved through the darkness to the light. The tracks hummed with energy, and when the pair of hired men—stepped onto the platform, 411 felt them like a spider feels a fly on his web. The silvery rattle their feet made on the brick was as loud to him as their guns. They were nearly lost now. The man who paid them had given them a map, but they could not read it. The Mytro had led them to La Rambla to be rid of them. 411 could smell their fear and confusion like a human smells rotten meat, dark and dead, with nothing new or good in it.

411 would have to move decisively. If the two intercepted the third, the children would be in grave danger. One of the older Nayzuns, 191, had told him of the time the humans had used the Mytro for violence, killing millions. Genghis Khan was one of the combatants, he recalled, and it was years before the stink of elephant dung left the Mytro's caves in Mongolia. Then the humans used wagons, forcing slaves to push them into the darkness. The wagon riders survived because they had maps. The slaves did not.

When it was time to stop the men and their butchery, the Nayzuns had to destroy each of the Mytro carts that carried Khan and his men through the steppes and into Europe. The Nayzuns burned them in their Hangar, the smoke thick against the ceiling. Many of the Nayzuns didn't survive that destruction. The humans again slowly forgot about the Mytro, and the Nayzuns were idle for centuries, working in silence on the rails, maintaining them for riders that never came. The Nayzuns thought they had been forgotten, but the Mytro had other ideas. Slowly, one at a time, the lines reopened, and by the time the Nayzuns were finished, the Mytro had snagged a new pair of discoverers, the Llorentes.

It wasn't until England learned to use the lines to colonize Africa that the cars were replaced by ornate trains, paid for at great cost by the East India Company. The humans negotiated with the Mytro in a language that had no words: the Mytro told them what it wanted, and the humans turned their effort into its wishes, in the same way, all those ages ago, the Nayzuns had begun to work for the Mytro and the Mytro slowly came to control them.

The humans were willful, but the Nayzuns had been willful as well. Ages before, the oldest Nayzuns said, the Mytro did not control the Nayzuns—the Nayzuns controlled the Mytro. When and where the power flipped was lost to time. In some ways, thought 411, it was better this way.

He was pulled out of his reverie by the voices of the two men. They were rustling a map, discussing where they had to go next. The sound as loud as waves crashing on the shore, at least to the Nayzun's sensitive ears. He wondered how the humans could be so crass, so bold. He rushed toward Barcelona, the tunnel elongating before him into a pinpoint.

He was nearly too late. The men jumped onto another train headed toward another station, closer to the center of the city. They got off. He could hear one of the men trying the door there, but it was shut. If the two men exited the Mytro, they would be lost to the rails.

Suddenly, 411 heard a new sound—the portable door opening somewhere in Barcelona. 411 knew that the portable door was a prize in itself, not to mention the arts that were used to build it. Whoever had found and used it was a true master of the rails, and now these men were about to control it.

The Nayzun knew that whatever was going on near La Rambla, it involved a great many powerful things, and 411, for a moment, felt something like fear. But his fears were quickly quashed as he remembered what Mytro was capable of.

The tunnel shunted him toward La Rambla, the darkness howling around him as he moved through the Mytro. Near the station where the men were fumbling with the door, 411 prepared himself. The air around him seemed to shimmer with menace, a cloud surrounding him and his long, impossible limbs.

CHAPTER TWENTY-TWO

Time to Get Away

They kept digging through the ripped papers and broken books.

Agata thumbed through a stack of yellowed papers—maps of some sort, but of the regular variety, showing old street systems in European capitals. There was Berlin but from before the war. Turtle had studied geography, and he knew that Sao Paolo was huge, but this map showed it as only a little bigger than Bay Ridge, with only a few main arteries and side streets. Penciled in on each map were a series of tiny *13*s dotting the major streets and some smaller locations. Were they Mytro stations?

As Turtle dug, he found a box of tourist guides. There had to be about 50 in the box, each for a different city—Hong Kong, London, Dubrovnik. He showed it to Agata. *13*s lined the major thoroughfares.

"Most summers we'd visit a different city. We'd live with one of my father's friends, and he'd walk around all day," she said. "He must have been making these maps."

"Interesting," said Mr. Kincaid. "I think he did a sort of caving. They call it urban spelunking."

"Spelunking?" asked Turtle.

"He'd go into tunnels and sewers and see how everything was put together. He once told me a story about how he discovered an entirely new Mytro line under Moscow. We'll have to ride it some time."

She flipped through some papers on the floor and pressed her hand against a broken picture of her father and mother standing in a train yard in Scotland.

"They took this photo before I was born. They were trainspotters. They used to go to train stations and watch the trains come in and leave. I guess now I know why," she said. "So what do we do now?"

"We're going to find your father's research, the Key and the map, and use it to get him back. I think we can find your mother, too," said Mr. Kincaid.

Turtle looked at Agata and then at the picture under her hand. She most resembled her mother with her high cheekbones, but her olive skin came from her darker father. Her father was nearly bald with just a small tuft of straight hair that brushed his ears and made its way around the back, so Agata's lustrous curls also most certainly came from her mother.

Turtle thought it must have been nice for her parents to see Agata grow up. The heaviness of the thought, like a chill, darkened the room for a minute until Mr. Kincaid snapped him out of his daydreaming.

"Our first step is to find the map, his personal one. A Mytratti's personal map is his prized possession. It's like a wizard's spellbook. I'll go downstairs and get us something to drink. You guys can keep digging," said Mr. Kincaid. "You know this place better than I would, right, Agata?"

"I've only been up here a few times these past few years though," she said.

"All I ask is that you try," said Mr. Kincaid.

He climbed down the circular stairs, and they heard him rummaging about in the kitchen. When they were sure he couldn't hear, Turtle turned to Agata and brought her close to him, holding her by the arm.

Putting his finger to his lips, he hushed her and brought her even closer. "If you find anything, hide it," Turtle told her in a whisper. "I don't know what's going to happen if we find anything here, and I don't know if we can trust Mr. Kincaid with it yet."

"Neither do I," said Agata. "I'm glad you're here though, Turtle."

Turtle swallowed hard. "I'm glad I'm here, too," he said, and they started sorting through the piles of Agata's father's research, searching for … what? Something that neither of them could describe but that was clearly important.

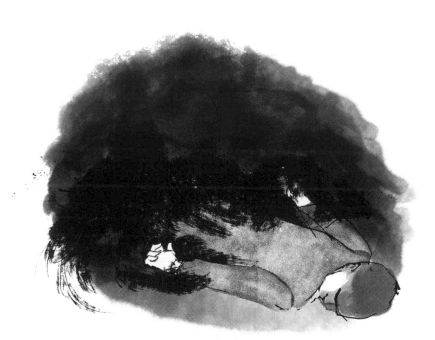

CHAPTER TWENTY-THREE

The Cold Dark

411 arrived at the small Rambla station just as the men were beginning to realize they were trapped. The taller of the two pushed at the door and found that it gave slightly. He pushed again, and suddenly he was whisked through to the other side. The Mytro had let him escape.

The other man rattled the door and rattled it again. Each time he opened the door, the wind from the tunnels slammed the door shut, trapping him. He tried to push a shoulder through, to chock the door with his foot, but he could not. It would open just a crack and then shut again. The Mytro was having its fun.

Slowly, the man realized he wasn't alone. He looked up at the

Nayzun, now coming down from the ceiling of the tunnel like a spider climbing down a wall. 411 had nothing to say to him.

The hired man turned white and stank of fear.

A train pulled into the small station and stopped with a screech. A ribbon of dust, disturbed by the wheels, puffed up at the Nayzun's feet. 411 stood by the door and gestured toward the train with his long fingers.

This is your train, the Nayzun said. The hired man stepped back. The Nayzun had a voice like a clattering on a set of distant tracks, the howl of a whistle through a tunnel, a distant crash. The man shook his head—No!—and the Nayzun was impassive. He stood before the human and gestured toward the train.

You can board the train and it will take you home, said 411. *You will never ride this train again. Or you can stay here and fight.*

411 had an inkling that the man would make the wrong choice. The Mytro seemed to know his mind better than the human did. All the humans ever wanted to do was fight. The train bell dinged and the doors closed.

The hired man pulled his pistol from his shoulder holster and aimed. The human fired, and the bullet thunked into the side of the departing train, splintering some of the wooden molding. He fired again, and the Nayzun was on the ceiling, his hands clinging to the surface of the tunnel using an energy that crackled like electricity and filled the room with the scent of ozone.

The Mytro did not take long to respond to this affront. 411 could hear the rails, steel wires in the dark, howling in anger. The darkness from both ends of the tunnel poured into the small station and began to roll over the trackbed and then up onto the platform. The man watched in horror as the darkness spread, covering the floor, crawling up the walls, inch by inch. The darkness flowed like water and began to lap at his shoes. The Mytro was angry and 411 heard it scream like bridge wires snapping in high winds or the sound of a dozen animals caught in a wire cage.

411 came down to be close to the man as he died. He screamed as the Nayzun grasped his wrist. The pain was clearly unbearable, and anger and fear froze on his face.

"Stop!" he yelled.

The woman, the girl's mother. Where?

"Manduria, Italy. The refugee camp. She's not hurt."

The Nayzun nodded sadly. *So you are trying it as well?*

"What? Trying what?"

Theft, said the Nayzun. *Slavery.*

411 let go of the man's wrist, and he crumbled onto the platform. His wrist was red but not injured. The darkness rose high enough to engulf the man. It rose over his head until he slowly disappeared into the darkness, his body covered inch by inch in a black flood. He had seemed passive during the experience, but perhaps fear shut his mouth and eyes. The darkness began to recede.

The Nayzun climbed along the ceiling and onto the top of an arriving train. The train's wheels sloshed through the darkness like a streetcar through a puddle. The darkness oozed off the front and sides of the train, leaving no residue. When the flood had receded, the man was gone.

In a way, 411 pitied the man, in the way a cat pities a mouse being devoured by a tiger. It was, in short, an unfair fight. The hired man never knew what was coming.

But 411 knew the simple rule: Everyone who took the Mytro by force or destroyed its foundations was punished. Of that 411 was certain.

CHAPTER TWENTY-FOUR

Map

They knew they were looking for something old. Turtle brushed through piles of paper, looking for faded antique documents. He couldn't find much, just some older subway maps of Berlin and Moscow and some newspaper clippings that looked to be about trains from the 1800s. Mr. Kincaid was still downstairs rummaging about in the kitchen, it sounded like. A pot clanged on the floor.

Turtle pushed through a few piles until he spotted something that looked interesting—a piece of paper, the color of weak tea, with fine printing on the edge. It was folded in half and clearly a Mytro map, but there wasn't much to distinguish it from other maps he had seen. He pulled at it a little and the corner crumbled slightly. Remembering the copy of Agata's map he had in his pocket, he began to compare the two. They were completely different. This map was far more precise and looked original. A sticky note on it read *"Para Agata."*

"Come over here," he said. Agata moved over to him quietly.

"Para Agata. It's for me," she said, eyes wide. She plucked the sticky note from the page and put it in her pocket. Then they unfolded the map.

This sheet was more ornate than the other ones and it seemed older. It was a topographic map, the kind that showed surface detail using shaded colors and heights from, Turtle supposed, sea level. It depicted the area around three large cities—Vienna, Prague, Budapest—connected by Mytro lines. Numbers in the corners of the cities looked like they pointed to separate maps, but for the first time, they noticed Mytro stops marked under water and in the middle of fields. There was a small inscription in the corner: *15 août 1914.*

"Is that a date?" asked Turtle.

"It's French. It's August 15," said Agata, thinking a bit.

Silence downstairs. Then they heard Mr. Kincaid's footsteps on the spiral staircase. Before they had a chance to react, he popped up, smiling. "What did we find?"

Turtle had no choice. Crumpling the map would probably destroy it, and Mr. Kincaid was right behind him. Turtle had to show it to him. As Turtle spread the map out on Agata's father's desk, Mr. Kincaid hunched over it for a closer look. His finger went to the date.

"August 15, 1914. That's a very important date to the Mytratti. That month, in Zurich, a group of them met to compare research. It was called the Last Conclave," said Mr. Kincaid. He looked at it closely. "This looks very professional. I've seen plates like this before but nothing of this quality. It's nicely printed."

"Did the Mytratti do it?" asked Agata.

"Most probably," said Mr. Kincaid.

"Where are the Mytratti now? Maybe they can help us," said Turtle.

"There aren't any left, really," said Mr. Kincaid. "They were a little too smart for their own good. No one has heard of them in decades. When the Mytratti met that August, they agreed to share all the information they had. Each was expected to add the stops they had found during their research. Agata's great-grandfather would have added the lines in Spain and Portugal while many of the professors—especially some of the rabbis—would have known these lines in the heart of Europe. This is mostly Prague and the surrounding towns."

Mr. Kincaid began to describe a scene from the previous century.

At a secret location believed to be a small, abandoned watch factory in Geneva, Switzerland, a group of 20 Mytratti had come together to share knowledge and ponder how the Mytro worked and what it could do for mankind. It was the beginning of World War I, August 1914, and the Mytro had suddenly become important again. Men of war saw the Mytro as an excellent way to transport troops and weapons. The pacifists saw grave danger. The group included some of the Llorente family, a young German patent clerk named Albert Einstein, a mathematician from England named David Hilbert, and many others. They began work on the great Mytro map and began to explore the notion of controlling the Mytro so it could not fall into the wrong hands.

The original Mytratti had laid the first tracks and created the first Mytro cars. They were based on the omnibus streetcar designs that were gaining popularity in European cities. Before that, the Mytro had beckoned travelers, much as it had when the Llorente brothers first found it. While the Mytro "worked," it was wildly disconcerting to be flung into the darkness by a wild wind. The Mytratti thought it would be much more comfortable to board a train in a civilized, well-maintained station.

George Brown, a Baltimore businessman who went on to found the B&O Railroad, laid the first tracks and hauled in the first Mytro car on a whim. The year was 1820, and Brown hoped the trains would carry passengers comfortably without the disconcerting feeling of being flung into the darkness by a wild wind. The tracks actually ran only the length of the stations and were cut off abruptly in the dark tunnels. They couldn't figure out how to lay tracks deeper into the darkness and it didn't seem to matter.

Luckily, this station-building experiment worked, and Brown began routing more cars through into the darkness. He built small stations using a group of workers, sworn to secrecy. The Mytratti protected the mystery of the stations with their lives, and once in a great while, men were thrown down into the tunnels to keep them quiet.

Their goal, at the beginning of the 19th century, was to harness the Mytro as a transportation system for mankind. Again and again, however, other groups moved in and took control of stations, capturing them and charging admission to ride. Every time the Mytro was to be revealed to the world, something would happen: a man would be pushed onto the tracks and sucked into the void, a fight would break out in a rarely used station, or a fire would gut a popular terminal. No one could be trusted with the Mytro, and so, again, after years of improvement, the Mytro was shut down for half a century.

Those who knew about the Mytro rarely spoke about it, but in 1914, the Mytro was slowly creeping back into public consciousness. Like a half-remembered dream, these new Mytratti did not question the existence of the Mytro, and tried to devise a method to control it. Like so many before them, they would fail, but in their search they began to learn far more about it than they ever expected.

Their first goal was to be able to shut down the Mytro when it was deemed too dangerous. Their second goal was to control the Mytro completely and to create a group of trained conductors to run the system and protect it. Many of the physicists understood that the Mytro operated well outside the realm of physics but how far outside no one was sure. Einstein and Alan Turing argued that the Mytro, like any physical object, had to follow the laws of nature. Many mystics in attendance, including a hooded man called Frater Perdurabo, believed the Mytro was metaphysical, something spiritual and more akin to a god than a train line. Neither party could agree, and in a way, it didn't matter. The Mytro simply *was*.

On that night, Perdurabo was dozing in the attic of the factory they had rented in Geneva when he was struck by a vision: a Key, the wards controlled by clockwork, that could send signals through the Mytro that would stop it and start it. Perdurabo imagined keyholes in every car that could shut them down permanently, perhaps even take control of the tunnels themselves.

Perdurabo never looked at the science of the thing, just the mystical patterns that the Mytro cast up before him. In his dream, he saw the shadow of the Key on a stone wall. He saw its patterns, the shape of its wards, the large head. A chain ran down from it and there was a crown, like a watch crown, to wind the Key like a clock. The Keys together would give the owner great power—at least that's what he imagined in his vivid dream.

The Mytro was a closed box, but Perdurabo was sure he had solved the mystery. He gathered the Mytratti together in a room— the scientists, the watchmakers, the astronomers—and asked for a piece of paper. An oil lamp guttered in the drafty warehouse and the Mytratti stood around him in a circle. He took up a long black fountain pen and sat, nib poised to paper, for a long time.

Slowly, slowly, with his eyes open but unseeing, his hand began to move, seemingly of its own accord. Outside, the cold Geneva evening grew colder as he scratched line after line on the cream-colored paper. In a near trance, he traced out two Keys—one long and thin, a skeleton key topped by a clockwork control system and another, shaped like a coin, designed to wind and set the Conductor's Key. In all, the machine-like key less resembled a skeleton key than clocks on the end of a long rod. When he was done, he threw the pen down and dropped backwards in exhaustion. The many scientists in the room laughed or stormed out while the watchmakers pored over the plans, discussing the finer points of the design.

"I will not be insulted by this hocus-pocus," wrote one prominent chemist that night in his diary.

The manufacture of the Key took a decade. Perdurabo changed the drawings multiple times, adding new read-outs and controls. It became more and more complex and now looked more like a pocket watch than a key. The Conductor's Key, as it was now called, held the real power. Now the Mytratti wanted to make multiple keys so they hired the best watchmakers in Switzerland to begin mass producing them.

The war interrupted the manufacture, and for a brief period, the Key—along with Perdurabo's plans—was lost. It reappeared in Warsaw and then travelled east as the Germans began to menace Europe again.

No one was quite sure what Perdurabo was doing or how his Key even worked. The first person to try the Key was Agata's grandfather who used it to shut down the entire Mytro from New York to Moscow. The only means of communication back then was wireless, and countless coded telegrams flew between continents confirming that the Mytro was not running.

13 SHUT NO TRAINS STOP. One telegram read, "13" being the code name for the Mytro, a sideways letter M with a line under it.

Many were upset with Perdurabo. The Mytratti wrote long, detailed letters to each other, discussing how they would take control of the Mytro if given the chance. Some would help refugees escape war-torn areas, and others would organize bucket brigades for parched farms. There had to be some way to use the Mytro for good, they argued.

Others wanted to use the Mytro for personal gain. They thought they could use it to smuggle soldiers over distant borders, and there was talk of using it as an ammunition transport for armies. Some Mytro stop doors could be altered to accommodate much larger vehicles, so they often thought of rolling huge carriages laden with goods and leading them out to the streets of a far-off trading post, ignoring local taxes and customs fees.

Perdurabo kept a diary into which he jotted ideas about the Mytro and its possible uses. But the Conductor's Key was still his crowning masterpiece.

Tales were told that Perdurabo died in Brussels or Bruges or sank in a submarine off the coast of Portugal after the war.

Rumor had it, however, that before he died, Perdurabo made one important visit. One night in 1945, the dark, strange man took the Mytro to visit the Llorente villa. He carried with him his diaries, maps, and the Conductor's Key. At some point during the war they had completed multiple copies of the Key. And they worked.

That was the last anyone had heard of the keys. The Llorentes lost their fortune, Perdurabo was gone, and the keys vanished into history. It would take half a century for them to be rediscovered.

"Then your father began to research it again, finding the old books and the old maps," said Mr. Kincaid. "We're the new Mytratti, your father, your uncle, myself, and a group of very rich men who see the potential in the Mytro. We're here to finally tame it, once and for all."

"Do you think all that is true? That story?" asked Agata.

"There are lots of tall tales told about the Mytro, and that's one of them. But I do know your father was closer than most to the truth, and whatever that truth was got him kidnapped," said Mr. Kincaid.

CHAPTER TWENTY-FIVE

Buscar Aquí

After listening to the story, Turtle's head felt cleaned out. All of that strange history, all of this new information.

"So this is one of the maps they used. Why would Agata's father have chosen only this part of it?" asked Turtle.

"Perhaps he discovered something?" said Mr. Kincaid.

"My father loved Prague. We've never been there as a family, but we have those old big mugs from old beer halls, so he must have visited," said Agata.

"Well, when I was first introduced to the Mytro by your father, he told me there were copies of copies of maps all over the world. He had a complete one and lots of other partial prints. The copy I use, for example, is one he gave me that covers New York and parts of Europe—just enough for me to get over to see your father. He kept much of his knowledge secret from the rest of us. From me, rather," said Mr. Kincaid, correcting himself. "He was never much for the community of seekers."

They began poring over the map, Mr. Kincaid looking over it with a magnifying glass he fished out of a pile of broken wood near the chair. Inch by inch, they took in every detail. They followed all the lines, and although they were drawn in different colored ink and by different hands, each of the stops was marked precisely with a tiny 13 and a set of letters. Something that looked like a little hill in the middle of a pasture was marked with "PCV" and a pair of coordinates.

The closer the lines came to the cities, the longer the codes. Each code was different—except for a few PCVs that seemed to appear over similar hills around the countryside. Sometimes they would include a name—"Mssr. Flaubert," for example—which suggested that the map included the names of the landowners. There were a few spots where the lines stopped and then started up again, an inch or so away. Using the scale, they could see that this Mytro map showed hundreds—if not thousands—of miles of track, crisscrossing and intersecting hundreds of times.

"There's one thing I don't get," said Turtle. "If all of these stops exist, why can't you just get on and say 'Paris?' to go to Paris?"

"The Mytro has lots of stops, but it never stops unless you tell it where. That's the problem. If you want to go to Paris, you have to know the station. Otherwise, you're stuck 'going' to Paris. It's a very specific tool."

Turtle thought about what Agata's uncle had told her: *Say 'Central Park South' when you board.*

"It would be like getting on a bus and telling the driver to take you to New York—except the Mytro would never let you off, right?" asked Turtle.

"Precisely," said Mr. Kincaid. "I'll be back shortly, friends. I need to make a phone call."

Mr. Kincaid walked back down the circular stairs, and Agata and Turtle went back to the map. A few minutes passed, then ten. The clock downstairs ticked quietly as they followed the lines from the edge of the page into the cities.

Agata gasped.

"Turtle," said Agata, "look at this."

Through the glass they were looking at a small, scrawled note. It consisted of a set of letters and then five numbers—1, 12, 28, 8, 21.

"What's that?" she asked. "It's my father's handwriting. I'm sure of it. He writes his sevens like that, with a little line in the middle. And his eights look like nines."

Turtle brought the magnifying glass close to the letters. He reached out for a pad of paper and Agata found him a pen. There in light pencil, barely visible among the tangle of drawn lines on the paper, was a series of random letters:

EQAFNUC 5, ITYAQGC, OQCDC

Then, under it, in ink, something else: *Buscar Aquí.*

"Seek here," said Agata. "That's what that means. That's my father's handwriting."

"So we look here," said Turtle, pointing to the underlined word.

In a flash, Turtle had written out the letters and numbers on a clean sheet of paper. The writing was near a circle that represented PRAGA on the map near the word *Čechy*, underlined twice.

"Does your dad like puzzles and things?" asked Turtle.

"He does," said Agata. "He also uses the computer a lot."

"So he'd probably have a way to encode some of his notes, I suppose. A way to keep this information out of the wrong hands."

"It's possible," said Agata. She looked at the map closely. "So this is Prague, in the Czech Republic. I remember it used to be called Czechoslovakia, around the time this map was created. I think it was World War I. But how is it coded?" asked Agata.

Turtle looked at the code for a minute, steeled himself, and nodded.

"I know what this is."

Turtle took a seat at Agata's father's desk and grabbed a clean sheet of printer paper. He copied the code from Mr. Kincaid's pad, leaving plenty of room to work. He also wrote down the numbers.

EQAFNUC 5, ITYAQGC, OQCDC
-1 13, 309, 820, 608

"So look: this first part is most definitely code. The letters repeat, so this is probably a substitution cipher, very simple. The number five also gives it away. If it were anything else, they would have coded the number as well. So you're basically substituting one letter for another. You just need to know the coded alphabet to decode this."

"Where did you learn this?"

"Just from some reading," said Turtle. "I like math. See how the writing is very quick, like someone didn't have a lot of time or maybe they just jotted it down? So either they copied it from something else or they were in a hurry. Hopefully that means the code isn't very difficult."

"Why would he encode his notes?" asked Agata.

"Leonardo da Vinci wrote everything backwards so people

couldn't read his notes. Maybe he knew your uncle would be able to figure it out? Your whole family are geniuses, right?" said Turtle.

"Not me," said Agata.

"Especially you. Plus you have smart friends," said Turtle. He felt embarrassed when he said it, but Agata hadn't noticed. "So look, if this is a substitution cipher, it can't be hard to crack. It's just a matter of finding the coded alphabet and the real one. If it's anything harder, though, we might be out of luck."

Turtle wrote the actual alphabet out on the page.

"You build an alphabet," said Turtle.

```
ABCDEFGHIJKLMNOPQRSTUVWXYZ
```

"What about odd letters?" asked Agata, thinking of the different letters she was accustomed to using in Spanish, like N.

"I don't know, but people don't usually use those in codes. You want a compact alphabet when building a cipher," said Turtle.

"So we have to imagine what this says," said Agata.

Turtle thought, counting the letters in each word.

"The last five letters might be the city, Praga." He connected the coded letters with the uncoded—or plaintext—alphabet.

```
ABCDEFGHIJKLMNOPQRSTUVWXYZ
C-----D--------O-Q--------
```

Turtle thought back to the books he read on codes and code-breaking. The key, all those books said, was patience and trial and error. He had patience, but he didn't have time for trial and error.

Agata pointed at the first letter. "C. Cechy," she said.

"Cechy … that's CEHY if this is a Caesarean cipher. You don't repeat letters."

He wrote out and erased the first few letters of "Cechy," without the odd letter.

```
ABCDEFGHIJKLMNOPQRSTUVWXYZ
CEHY--D--------O-Q--------
```

"Interesting," said Turtle. "Now we have to finish it. The key is short but we still have to be careful. You just fill in the rest of the letters that you didn't use in the key, in order."

He wrote out the rest of the letters one by one, double-checking. Butterflies rose in his stomach as the code came into focus. He was right. It was simple, easy to remember, and easy to solve—but just hard enough if you didn't know what you were doing.

```
ABCDEFGHIJKLMNOPQRSTUVWXYZ
CEHYABDFGIJKLMNOPQRSTUVWXZ
```

He finished the alphabet with a flourish and dropped the pen on the table.

"If this is right, I think we may have solved it," said Turtle. Turtle began scribbling furiously, crossing out and replacing letters in the coded message. It took him a minute:

```
BREHOVA 5, JUDERIA, PRAGA
```

"Juderia?" asked Agata.

"Do you have Internet here?" asked Turtle.

Agata nodded. Turtle straightened out a monitor that was lying facedown on the desk—the other monitor on the floor was shattered—and checked the connections. They turned on the computer, and after it booted up, he searched for the address Brehova 5. Immediately, a map appeared showing a maze of streets in Old Town Prague, the heart of an ancient Central European city.

"It hasn't changed enough that the addresses are much different. It looks like it's in a hotel. Brehova 5."

The floor creaked behind them. They had been so engrossed in the puzzle they hadn't noticed Mr. Kincaid had quietly climbed the stairs and joined them. He was beaming.

"Indeed it does, Paul. Indeed it does. That, my friend, was one of the most fascinating feats of mental gymnastics I've seen in anyone your age. I'm impressed," said Mr. Kincaid, patting Turtle on the shoulder. "And it looked like fun."

Turtle and Agata turned around, stricken. They stared at Mr. Kincaid. Turtle tried to grab the paper—or at least commit it to memory. *Brehova 5, Brehova 5* he repeated over and over.

"Sadly, what has to happen next won't be," said Mr. Kincaid.

Turtle heard movement on the stairs.

"Lads," said Mr. Kincaid.

One of the men who shot at Agata on the train walked up the stairs into Agata's father's study. He was standing with a stranger, a man with close-cropped hair and a red, splotchy face. He was carrying a stun gun, its silver barbs glinting with menace in the lamplight.

"'Tis quite a walk up those stairs," said the red-faced man. "I'm out of breath!"

"Children, this is Mr. Goode. He's going to help us find your parents."

"Good day, children," said Mr. Goode.

Turtle felt sick. *Brehova 5,* he repeated to himself. *Brehova 5. Prague.*

CHAPTER TWENTY-SIX

Lay Your Cards Out

Turtle looked to Mr. Goode, then down at the stun gun. It lay in his hand like a sleeping snake, not pointed at them but hanging, lazily, like Mr. Goode forgot it was even there.

The other man, a blonde with a scruff of a beard, had been wearing a mask when he saw him in the subway, but Turtle remembered his dark, scuffed boots.

"This is my associate from the military—or formerly in the military. Mr. Adams, let me introduce you to Agata Llorente and Paul Fulton."

"A pleasure," said Mr. Adams with a rich, slow British accent. "I'm Martin. Martin Adams. And, incidentally, we didn't mean to fire at you, dearie," said Mr. Adams. "Trigger slipped."

Mr. Goode grinned. "I assure you, dear lady, we mean no harm unless, of course, there is a problem. I'm not the threatening type, Agata, but, as your father knows, we have been looking long and hard for the things he possesses, and so we're going to do what we need to do. Is that understood?"

Agata looked at him impassively.

"All's fair in love and war, and I understand your reticence to work with us. But work with us you will. This is the plan," said Mr. Goode. "You're going to go with this man here, once his associate arrives. They will take you to your mother, Agata. They'll take Paul here as well. You'll stay where I put you for a few days until I find the second half of the Conductor's Key, and if all goes according to plan with no rash moves, we'll let you go. We'll tell your grandmother where you are, of course. We'll tell the truth but tell it slant, as they say. No use in alarming her about the Mytro and Barcelona. She'll think you're being kept against your will. How does that sound?"

"My father trusted you!" exclaimed Agata. Turtle grabbed her hand and she squeezed it tightly. "He told me I could trust you, Mr. Kincaid."

"You can just let us go. Tell us where Agata's mom is and let us go," said Turtle.

"I would, but you two know the Mytro too well, and I'd worry that you'd be able to point in our direction people we don't want interrupting. We'll take your map, to be certain, but I'd rather have a few unencumbered days to work."

Turtle ran through the situation in his head, the same way he ran the cipher. It was convoluted but clear: whatever the Mytro had done, it had put Turtle into Agata's path and, unfortunately, into Mr. Kincaid's. But how did Mr. Kincaid know who had found Agata?

Turtle could have kicked himself for being so stupid. He had been wearing his Manhattan Friends gym T-shirt when he opened the door for Agata back in the park. The men must have seen him, and Mr. Kincaid would trace it back to Nick and Nate. One quick call and Mr. Kincaid knew everything he needed to know.

"Where is her father?" asked Turtle.

"Her father is a special case. Even we don't know where he is. I assure you he isn't in our custody," said Mr. Goode.

Mr. Kincaid walked over to the door propped against the wall of her father's study. Mr. Adams reached into his pocket and pulled out two white pieces of plastic, about as wide as pipe cleaners but twice as long.

"Now, if you'd be so kind as to hold out your hands for Mr. Adams, he'll put you in cuffs and we can get you to your mother."

"Not too tight, Martin," said Mr. Kincaid, but Mr. Adams pulled the cuffs taut on Turtle's wrists, the white plastic cutting into his skin. Then he zipped them over Agata's. She winced but said nothing. When she moved, he noticed the leather cord hanging around Agata's neck.

Turtle's mind raced: Agata still had the other part of the

Conductor's Key. Mr. Goode didn't know she had it. He thought it was still in Prague. Mr. Adams gave the cuffs another tug.

"Stop that, not so tight," yelled Turtle.

"Sadly I can't loosen them once they're on. We'll cut them off soon enough. If you would lead the way, Paul," said Mr. Goode. "But if you would, do me one final kindness, Mr. Kincaid. Could you take possession of what we've been looking for?"

Mr. Kincaid reached out toward Agata's neck. He pulled back her shirt collar to reveal the leather cord holding the other half of the Conductor's Key. He reached out to the office desk littered with papers and books and plucked a pair of scissors from the mess. Then, with a quick snip, the key was his.

"You knew?" asked Agata.

"I did know and I was quite disappointed when you didn't tell me in the restaurant. Much of this could have been avoided if you had never left Brooklyn, Turtle. You could have both been home. Instead, we have this sorry state of affairs."

"Quite sorry," said Mr. Goode.

"Friends, our train has arrived." Mr. Goode opened the portable station with a flourish just as the next train roared into view. The three men—Mr. Adams with his gun drawn, Mr. Goode with his stun gun lying idle at his side, and the timid Mr. Kincaid—stepped over the threshold into the small space. Mr. Kincaid helped the children through the door, righting them as they fell forward slightly. The Mytro train doors opened. Agata screamed.

CHAPTER TWENTY-SEVEN

Echoes

For a moment Turtle couldn't understand what he was seeing. Standing in the middle of the car, framed by the open train car door, was a tall, thin creature with long legs and arms. The air in the room seemed to fall still as they all took in the sight.

It had long, thin fingers and skin that was almost pearlescent. In the gas lamp, glints of yellow reflected on its long, thin face. It had dark sockets where its eyes would be and small holes where ears would be. There was no mouth.

But it spoke to them.

Do not be afraid, it said. The voice was a sort of buzzing rattle, like a train rushing to a stop and then chugging up again. It was the voice of the rails.

The thing reached through the car door and pulled the children away from Mr. Martin and Mr. Goode. The two men stared silently as the children were drawn farther into the car and the door began to close. The men were as stunned as Turtle was, he realized. The thing had a hold of him and Turtle felt a buzz, like electricity, ride his arm through his spine and out his feet.

The thing's long arms enveloped them, and Turtle smelled something like dust and something else like oil.

They were inside the car now, and he just had a few moments to take in the station itself. There was something written over the platform in what Turtle recognized as Hebrew. Then the train door closed in front of him, trapping the three men on the outside. He heard pounding on the other side, and shouting. He could see them gesticulating through the doors.

Immediately, it all became clear.

"What's happening?" screamed Agata.

"You mentioned the Nayzuns, remember?" said Turtle. "I think this is one."

The thing looked over at them. The train dinged twice and prepared to roll.

The thing pointed at the seats.

"Stop them!" yelled Mr. Goode, but his voice was drowned out by the rising pitch of the wheels as the train began to exit the station.

Mr. Adams lifted his gun to fire, but he shot wildly and it hit the back wall of the train with a thud. Inside the small station the blast from the gun's muzzle was deafening, and all Turtle could hear was a high-pitched whine and something grating and metallic. Mr. Adams fired again, but by now the train was far away from them, floating in the dark that enveloped it as completely as water.

"Nayzun," she said.

Yes, said the thing, his face immobile, the voice coming from nowhere and, at the same time, seeming to come from inside their heads. *I am a Nayzun, a Nameless One. I am 411.*

"Is that your name?" asked Turtle.

No, but it is sometimes easier to have an identifier when your charges tend to require them. It is not a name like yours, but it is sufficient. But let's not talk of that now. Those men are sent to hurt you.

"Yes, I suppose," said Turtle.

Then you are safe now, said the Nayzun.

The train rattled on through the dark. They weren't stopping, it seemed, and the Nayzun relaxed slightly, its long spine arching a bit as it turned to address them.

You are the children, it said in a way that suggested it wasn't a question.

"You knew about us?" Agata asked.

The rails spoke of you. The Mytro knows you are important. We do not know the mind of the Mytro, but we are aware of its desires.

They stood, quiet, until the thing took a step back. The noise of the train racketed around them as they rode. None of them had thought of a destination, so they seemed to be suspended in the dark, hurtling but not moving.

I sense that you fear me. I am here to protect you, it said, and for the first time Turtle realized it wasn't speaking to him but through his head with a sound like a piece of paper over a loudspeaker or the hum of train wheels on old rails.

"Are you an alien?" asked Turtle.

If it helps for you to think of me that way, then I am. Please understand that the Mytro is quite different from your perception of the universe. The Mytro is something very old, and we have always worked in it. We make the rails whole, the stations habitable. We make the Mytro happy.

The Nayzun looked at them both and nodded slowly.

Please, sit, children, you are tired and full of questions. You are safe.

"I'm Paul and this is Agata. We're looking for her mother."

We will find her. But first you must go get the Conductor's Key. It is important that we have it.

"But Mr. Goode has part of it," asked Agata.

He has the winder. There are many of those. We need the real clockwork key, the Key of the Mytratti.

Your mother is safe, girl, and we know where she is. However, your father, the researcher, is very far away and will be much more difficult to retrieve. I believe once you have the Conductor's Key you'll begin to understand what you're up against and what tools you have at your disposal, said 411.

Please, do not fear, said 411. *I am here to help.*

"That's what the last guy said," spit Turtle, looking out into the dark.

Please, said the Nayzun. *Listen.*

The Nayzun gestured toward the darkness outside the window.

There is something happening to the Mytro. My kind has maintained it since your world was young, and we will continue to do its work until the last planet is dust. We are the ones who work, and it is the one who traverses space to bring things into proper alignment.

You are part of a much bigger plan, and I can tell you very little of that plan right now. I am too young to know it, but I fear it has a great deal to do with both of our worlds. The Mytro is angry. It is changing, and there are men who would tame it while it is weak. If they attempt this, the Mytro could collapse or close or change, and even we Nayzuns fear that change.

Your father was hard at work, trying to understand that change, and he shared too much with the men who are after you now. They sensed a weakness in the Mytro, something they could use for their own ends although I do not believe they understand just what they seek. The creation of the Key gave humans far too much power over the Mytro, and we Nayzuns believe the Mytro gave you the key in order to free itself from whatever bonds hold it. Like the Nayzuns, the Mytro seems to have a master.

As for the men, they are far away. I must take you to find the Key as quickly as possible, and then we must go to the oldest ones, in our Hangar, and learn where we are to go next. We can find your mother, Agata, as we travel, but she is less important to this plan.

"So where is Mr. Kincaid? Where can we call the police?" asked Agata.

The Mytro is not very hospitable to strangers and few know that it exists—let alone understand its vagaries. I'm afraid to say that the rails will dispense their own form of justice when the time comes, and it is my hope that everyone but the perpetrators, including yourselves, will come out spared. So we will go to Prague, and there you will find the Key, and then we must see what the Mytro wants next.

"We thank you, 411, for finding us," said Turtle. Now that he took a closer look at the tall gray creature, he realized how beautiful it looked. There seemed to be no bones in its arms, yet they were sturdy and solid, and there were no ribs peeking through its chest. It was shaped like a human, to be sure, but it was more than a human, and Turtle almost expected it to wink away at any moment. It was a human torn away from the world, ripped and elongated like starlight.

"Did you think things would turn out like this?" asked Agata.

"Never, but it's fun."

"They're shooting at us," said Agata.

"And they keep missing."

With that, 411 moved his hand, and suddenly the train lurched forward faster and faster, hurtling through the dark and into a brightly lit station that materialized around them like a complex origami.

We have a unique relationship with the Mytro, said 411. We are not bound by some of its rules, or at least the rules that have been put into place to make the rails easier for you to understand.

"So everything about the Mytro is fake? It doesn't really look like a train?" asked Agata.

Perhaps you are right, said 411. *However, I do not see it as a train to begin with, which makes it hard for me to explain to you.*

"What does it look like to you?"

Entropy, said 411. *Endless change. A field of energy that we all move through. This, children, is your stop.*

Turtle lifted his hands off his lap, straining at the zip tie.

"Can you untie us first?"

CHAPTER TWENTY-EIGHT

Na Karlově Mostě

The Nayzun held up his hands as if showing them something—the Nayzun had no thumbs.

"I have a little knife in my back pocket," said Agata. She stood up and hopped around so Turtle could reach in to fish it out. He felt slightly embarrassed and the blood rushed to his face, but he found the little red knife, opened it, and cut her zip tie. Then she cut his.

The doors chimed open and the Nayzun motioned for them to exit.

"Where will you go?" asked Agata.

I will return to the portable door station in your father's study in an hour your time. You are safe in there. Just say your address and you will be taken there.

"Thank you, 411, for helping us," said Turtle. From somewhere in the station came a loud creaking noise, as if the tracks were moving. The Nayzun shifted, his large form tilting slightly to one side as if moving away slightly from them. Then it turned its head back to face them.

You are welcome. The Nayzun motioned for them to leave. *Please go. The sooner you find the Key, the sooner we can move you to safety.*

They left the car and the train rolled away. They stood in the small station and looked around. There were two exits, the doors only about three feet high. The sign above both read "Staré Masto Most Karluv, Praga." The right door read "Pod Karlovým mostem," and the left one read "Na Karlově mostě."

"Which one?" asked Agata.

"When in doubt, always go right," said Turtle. Agata shrugged and opened the door, releasing a wall of water that rushed through and out into the trackbed. Turtle and Agata leaped out of the way just in time, and the door slammed shut as a rush of sludge threatened to pour through it.

"Left, I think," said Turtle.

"Left," said Agata.

They pushed through the small door and walked into crisp, fresh air.

The station was empty—for a moment. A minute later, and unbeknown to them, another train rolled into the station and a man in a long raincoat, his face shadowed by flickering gas lamps, disembarked, waited a moment, and then took the left door to follow them into the bustle of Prague.

CHAPTER TWENTY-NINE

The Conductor's Key

The Mytro door opened behind a wooden box full of sand. A well-used shovel clattered over when they came through, but no one turned to look at a pair of kids clamoring out of nowhere. They were on a bridge lined with tall sandstone statues. Kings and queens stood stolidly overlooking the dark brown river. The slow-moving crowd of people, intent on getting photos of the spires and brickwork of Old Town Prague, were clicking away with cameras and cell phones while hawkers on the bridge sold caricatures and jewelry.

There was a bite of cold in the Prague air. The sun was already going down over the river, and the city lights were winking on. Agata pulled out her cell phone and pulled up a map application. A few seconds later, a virtual pin dropped to their location, and the phone dinged with messages.

"Who is it?" asked Turtle.

"It's the phone company. They send texts when you land in a new country. What they think about me getting from Barcelona to Prague in a second I have no idea. But no messages from my uncle."

She waited, as if to see if any would come. They didn't.

"This is the Charles Bridge," she said. "Brehova is down that way."

Old Town Prague looked like something out of a fairy tale. The brick buildings were wonderfully ornate with small figures adorning many of the facades. Leering gargoyles looked down over the cobbled streets, and signs advertised kebab, souvenirs, and ghost tours.

They followed the online map a few more twisted blocks until they were on Brehova Street. When they looked up, they spotted a small restaurant, U Vltavy, and a line of white stone buildings, more ornate in style, lined the rest of the street.

"It's there," said Agata. She pointed to a large, yellow and cream brick building offset by bright white decorations.

They stood there for a moment before Agata turned to Turtle. "How many stories does this building have?"

Turtle counted then double-checked. "Four," he said.

"Exactly. Do you remember the numbers on my father's paper?"

Turtle produced Mr. Llorente's map.

"So look at these numbers," she said. "They're under 400 and there's a '−1' here, which means the basement."

"So ...," said Turtle, thinking.

"So they're room numbers."

"The first one's in the basement, right? Let's go there," said Turtle.

In front of the hotel stood a tall, thin man with blonde hair. He wore a black shirt and black pants and was holding the door open for people walking up to the hotel.

"How do we get past the doorman?" asked Turtle.

"That's the easy part," she said.

Agata grabbed Turtle's hand, and they crossed the street into the glow cast by the lights inside the posh hotel. The doorman said something in Czech and then English.

"Can I help you?" he asked.

"My grandmother is here," said Agata.

"Is she a guest of the hotel?" asked the doorman.

"Of course," said Agata.

"Then go to the front desk. They can call her down for you," said the doorman.

"She said she was in the basement. Is there a basement here?" asked Agata.

"Floor 1 on the elevator," said the doorman. "But the basement is just the offices and cleaning supplies. Don't go down there," he called back, already occupied with a woman leading a tiny poodle through the revolving door. He ran over to help the woman when the little dog yelped and was nearly snatched up in the door.

"Easy as pie. Nobody cares about people in a hotel," she said. "I've been in a lot of them."

"I've seriously never been to any," said Turtle.

Turtle and Agata rushed into the brightly lit hotel lobby. The hotel was beautiful, the marble floors polished to a high shine and the furniture all rich, dark, and modern. A woman at the front desk smiled at them and picked up a phone, ignoring them a moment later.

"Elevators," said Agata, grabbing Turtle's hand. Another chill rose up the back of his spine. They came to the elevators and jammed the down button. The doors opened immediately with a curt *ding* and they were inside. A moment later, the doors opened.

"This is P. This isn't 1," said Turtle.

"Maybe we can go farther down," said Agata.

This floor was mostly empty with piles of sheets and pillows dumped into big cloth bins and something that sounded like a kitchen a few feet away from the elevator entrance. It looked like one large room, with a few smaller rooms that looked like break areas for the staff at the far end.

Next to the elevator was a darker elevator door that was much wider and much older than the elevator they had ridden.

"That has to be a staff elevator," said Agata. She walked over to it. Her finger pinned down something scratched into the paint. The number 13.

"Bingo," she said. "Is that the right word? My mom says it when she spots something she lost."

"Bingo is right," said Turtle, smiling. They were inside the elevator before anyone noticed.

The quiet was immense in the sub-basement. The upper basement had looked relatively new, with a fine tile floor and a clean, astringent quality to the air. Here, in the lower storage area—unused by all accounts—it felt cramped and dirty.

To the left of the elevator was a door marked WC, and another room, its door ajar, was lined with lockers. It appeared to be the men's changing room. Someone inside was rustling about with a bag, and Agata and Turtle quietly moved past the door deeper into the cellar. This floor was much bigger than the one above it, which suggested it was the older of the two. It was dimly lit with light bulbs where the upper basement was awash in fluorescent light. If there was a place to hide something in the hotel, this was it.

They went all the way down to the end of the hall to a large, wooden double door. It was locked. Then Agata noticed something.

"Look at the room numbers," she said.

"There are none," said Turtle.

"Except that one," she said, pointing to a room on the right side of the hall. It was labeled, in black marker, with the number 13.

They tried the door and it opened, the hinges quiet.

The musty smell told them this area hadn't been disturbed in a while. There were old leather chairs stacked up in a jumble and a set of tablecloths that looked as if they had seen a bit too much tomato sauce. They heard the boiler farther away, in the darkness at the far end of the room. Somewhere above, a toilet flushed and the rush of water roared through some pipes above them.

Agata took out her cell phone and tapped a button that turned on the built-in flash. She used it as a flashlight, sweeping the area in front of them.

"So it's in this room, I guess. Unless there's another Mytro station, right?" asked Turtle.

Agata raised the flashlight, aiming it at the walls. There was no sign or mark, just a uniform wall made of large, carefully cut stone bricks. They walked gingerly along the walls, stepping over broken furniture and a couch that looked like it had seen better days. Near the back corner, someone had cleared the debris into orderly stacks.

They trailed their hands slowly along the wall, feeling for changes in the surface. Turtle thought of the rock wall in Central Park that fell in with a soft push.

Under the harsh light of the phone's LED, all the stones looked the same. Agata flashed the light across the wall again and turned around to look at the organized furniture.

"My dad did this, I think," she said. "He was always cleaning. His attic, before it was trashed, was so tidy."

The flashlight rolled over the dark wood and caught the wall again.

"Pull back a little. Aim the light right here," Turtle said, tapping a point on the wall.

Agata moved back and aimed where Turtle was pushing. In the brick wall, clearly delineated, was a set of bricks that was lighter than the others, as if they had been cleaned. They were shaped like the letter A.

Turtle pressed one then another, completing the A. They all clicked back a bit with his touch. There were eight in all—three for either side of the A, one for the top, and one for the crossbar. Turtle pressed all eight.

Slowly, the wall rolled inwards and then back. It was a station, bright and new, made of blindingly polished steel—long sheets of it, riveted together.

The ceiling was gently sloped to the edge of the tracks, which were new as well and set into dark concrete studded here and there with some sort of glowing mineral. The tunnel disappeared into darkness on either side.

It was a unique station, to be sure. Above the door, which was now closing after them, a name was etched into the metal: "Agata Station, Prague."

"What the heck?" asked Turtle. "Did your dad do this?"

"I have no idea," she said. "I don't know how he could. Turtle—look," said Agata. She pointed and then ran to a box near a far wall they hadn't noticed. It was metal, specially designed with a close-fitting lid. It was locked tight and a dial beckoned.

"The numbers," said Turtle. "We didn't write them down."

"I remember them. 12 28 08 21. My birthday, then my mom's," said Agata.

She turned the dial clockwise then counterclockwise, hitting the numbers. Two more turns and she tugged the lid softly. It lifted up on hidden hinges.

There, settled in a soft silk pillow, was a large, ornate key. The fob looked like a pocket watch and a set of dials and buttons studded the length of it. The tip of the key was ornately carved, curlicues twisting into geometric shapes. It was so brightly polished that it seemed to glow. As she lifted it out of the box, it jingled slightly, like wind chimes. It was still alive, still wound. A bright button on the top could activate it, but Agata didn't want to touch it.

This was the Conductor's Key. She lifted it from the box and held it, staring amazed at its complexity.

"Look," said Turtle. "There's one more!"

Under the shiny key was another darker key, one that looked older and less polished. It was the original.

Behind them the door started to open and they both turned. Agata grabbed the old key from the box and stuffed it into a front pocket as a tall man dressed in a dark coat and beret pushed into the bright station.

CHAPTER THIRTY

Mr. Partridge

The man doffed his beret and looked around, blinking. He was tall and thin with sunken cheeks and a sharp nose. His watery blue eyes glinted behind small, gold-wire spectacles. He was young, younger than Mr. Kincaid, and nearly bald, his hair cut short against his scalp where it still sprouted softly like gray and black moss.

"Good evening, Agata and, er, Agata's friend," he said. "I'm Niles Partridge, your father's assistant." He spoke with a soft British accent.

Turtle and Agata looked at him, startled. Agata turned to see if a train was coming, but the station was quiet. They were trapped. After Mr. Kincaid and his friends, there was no way they would trust another stranger.

"If you're his assistant, why don't I know you?" asked Agata.

"Your father and I worked in London together. He would visit me during the day. I kept copies of his research, out of sight. I'm a former student of his from Cambridge. May 12 will be the third anniversary of my employment—if I recall correctly. I never met you or your mother. He said it would be safer that way."

"Yeah sure," said Turtle. He balled his fists, ready to fight. "You're with Mr. Kincaid."

"I'm not. I don't know a Mr. Kincaid but if he's with Goode then I'm sorry you had to meet him. I'm also sorry that you got mixed up in this. I've just been to your home and seen the damage … and found the directions. I was supposed to help your father and mother if it ever came to this, and it seems you've beaten me to it."

"How do we know that?" asked Agata. "You've never been to our house."

"I have been upstairs when you weren't home. I'd come in from the Piccadilly Circus station near my apartment and meet your father in his study. I know I can't prove it, but I know a lot about you. I gave your father the train lamp that you have in your room. I know he loves you very much and carries a picture of you as a baby in his wallet. I know your father calls you his heaven. *Mi cielo*."

Agata shivered. Turtle looked over at her and she nodded slightly.

Turtle looked at her, confused. "So what do you want?"

"Your father," Mr. Partridge said to Agata, "my friend, told me that if anything happened to him, I was to keep an eye on these Keys but he didn't tell me where they were. I followed you here after those men lost you. He built this place as a sort of storage space for the Conductor's Keys and kept the secret from me. He is the one who made the wall outside and the letter *A* from bricks. I'm glad you found your way. I'm very impressed. I was worried you'd be lost. "

"Why the code? Why do that?" asked Turtle.

"We created the code to hide the locations of stations in various cities. It's fairly simple—we just used the country as a key—but it worked. I told him we should have used computers more, but he was always afraid of hackers. Now that this has happened, I'm glad we did it his way and not mine. Do you still have the other half of the key?"

"The necklace? No, Mr. Kincaid took it," said Agata.

"Oh dear. A bother. I trust you've found your way around the Mytro well enough with his maps? They're very thorough."

"411 also helped us," said Agata. "He's waiting for us."

"411?" asked Mr. Partridge.

"A Nayzun," she said.

Mr. Partridge nearly sank to his knees.

"Oh dear," he squeaked. "I see."

CHAPTER THIRTY-ONE

The Breach

411 rode the Mytro through station after station. He had sensed the children somewhere in Prague, but he couldn't pinpoint their location after they left the bridge. Perhaps they were at the hiding place. Whatever power the girl's father used to build the station was also invisible to him. Only the Mytro knew where the children were, and it wasn't telling.

Even so, the Mytro trusted him. 411 had been there when the first Conductor Keys were made. The men who made them hadn't seen him, but the Mytro had sent him to watch their progress. It was endearing to see the humans struggle and succeed. It was beautiful to see them begin to understand something so complex with their limited minds. When they nearly harnessed the Mytro, it looked as if they would leave the instincts of their Neanderthal forbears behind.

Sadly it never came to pass.

The rails sang for a moment. The children had found the keys.

The children must close the Breach, sang the rails.

The Breach? asked 411, and then he realized what the Mytro meant. For months there had been a strange background noise on the rails, as if something were slowly cracking. The Nayzuns had ignored it—there were plenty of strange things on the rails—but now 411 understood. The Breach, the great power. If the humans broke the Breach, the Mytro would change forever.

The rails sang, telling 411 where to go.

411 sang back. His voice rang through the darkness and the Mytro answered. In a moment he knew where the children had to go. He simply had to find them now before the gunmen did.

CHAPTER THIRTY-TWO

Stuck in the Dark

"You saw a Nayzun?" said Mr. Partridge.

"He's been helping us. We're about to go meet him," said Agata. She stopped herself before she said where. She didn't want to give too much away.

"We had been discussing Nayzuns for years, your father and I. We were unsure if they existed," said Mr. Partridge.

"Oh, they exist," said Turtle, knowingly. "What do you know about them?"

"As far as we can tell, they maintain the tracks but no one has seen them in centuries. There are many legends," said Mr. Partridge.

"Good or bad?" asked Agata.

"I couldn't tell you precisely. They're not a kind and loving lot in the old stories, to be sure," said Mr. Partridge. "They equate them with devils. Please, let me come with you. I can't make you trust me, Agata. I know you're confused right now, but I've been tasked to help," he said.

"We're not confused," she said. "We're angry. This is a mess. My uncle and my parents are gone. We were nearly shot, and now we're supposed to go with you?"

"I can't make you, but I'd actually prefer you to think of it as me going go with you, just to help," he said.

"We're doing fine on our own. We need to meet 411."

"I'd like to meet it as well," he said.

Turtle and Agata looked at each other.

"Show us what you have in your coat," said Turtle with a force that surprised him. "There have been too many people with guns around us recently."

Mr. Partridge opened his coat and revealed a white button-down shirt, stained yellow near the collar, and dark pants. He pulled a notebook out of his breast pocket and then a wallet. He held them out for Turtle to take and then pulled out a red pen without a cap.

"I'm a teacher," said Mr. Partridge. He pointed at the stain. "And that is probably a curry I ate. I've been in a bit of a panic."

"Where's your phone?" asked Turtle.

"I don't have one. I'm one of the last not to have one. I never liked them—nasty business."

Turtle handed back his things. They seemed so forlorn, as did Mr. Partridge. He wasn't cocky, like Mr. Kincaid.

"Can he come along?" asked Agata.

Turtle looked at him and nodded in agreement. "He can come."

A few moments later a train whooshed into the station and stopped. The doors opened and they boarded.

"Barcelona …," said Agata, unsure. "The portable door."

She recited her address.

The train dinged and rolled into the dark. It picked up speed and the window glass rattled in its frames. The trio sat, Agata near the door, Mr. Partridge tapping his foot noisily on the wooden floor. Turtle flanked him, watching him out of the corner of his eye.

Then they stopped. The whole train seemed to freeze, and the clattering ceased. They were stuck in the dark. Turtle stood but was unsure where he was. He reached out and felt the brass rail along one side of the train and, hand-over-hand, tried to move to where he thought Agata would be.

"What did you do?" he yelled at Mr. Partridge. His voice sounded hollow, oddly empty, as if the air were thinner.

"I didn't do a thing," said Mr. Partridge from somewhere to Turtle's left.

Turtle grappled in the dark and reached out until Agata finally grabbed his hand. He couldn't see her, but she was there.

"Don't move. Nobody move," said Agata.

Then the Nayzun appeared in the dark, his bioluminescent skin casting a cold blue glow on the train.

I've stopped you here. It's not safe at your father's office. There are more men there. I will take you to where we need to go.

The train began to move.

"Nayzun," whimpered Mr. Partridge. He'd been standing but plopped back down and out of sight. The pearlescent light cast by the creature did not reach him, but Turtle could hear Mr. Partridge pull out his notebook and begin to scribble furiously in the dim light.

Good evening, Mr. Partridge. It is a pleasure. I have watched you for a number of years, said 411. *You can trust this man, children.*

"Well, that's good," said Agata. "He's been dying to meet you."

As they started moving, the lights came back on, and Mr. Partridge stood suddenly, nearly falling over. He reached out his hand eagerly but the Nayzun looked at him. A twinkle of blue pulsed through the creature's body, and it bowed its head slightly toward the nervous professor.

"I've waited years for this," said Mr. Partridge.

I am 411. I am one of the oldest of my clan. I've been tasked to close the Breach that you and Mr. Llorente have been studying.

Mr. Partridge let his hand drop.

"So it's real, the Breach?"

That is not our word for it, but we know of it and we know Mr. Goode and his men are working diligently on it. They've already carved out a large space for their work, and if their plan comes to fruition, they would be far out of your jurisdiction in a few weeks.

"What's the Breach?" asked Agata.

"Your father and I discovered a huge station under Barcelona. It was created the same way your father created the Prague station, using a Key. However, it was never completed and it is very unstable. Mr. Goode is trying to finish it for heaven knows what reason. But the Breach could manifest itself in *our* reality, flattening most of the city."

"So it's a station that could take up space?" asked Turtle. "What does that mean?"

"Think of the Mytro as a cake. Before you bake it, it's a mass. No holes. Once you bake it, little bubbles form, breaking up the mass. The Mytro, as it is now, is the cake before it's baked. There are *potential* bubbles in the batter, but you can't tell where they'll form. If the Mytro station Mr. Goode is mussing about in actually manifested into our reality, it would collapse most of the city—it's that large."

"He needs the Key to stabilize it," said Agata.

"Exactly," said Mr. Partridge. "He nabbed your parents as leverage, hoping you'd bring the Keys to him."

I will take you to where your mother is, Agata. While you are there, you must also get the winder from Mr. Goode. It is imperative. Then we will find your father. Keep the keys safe.

"Then you take one, Turtle," she said. "It's yours. You may need it. Then we need another winder."

"Your father hid the other winder," said Mr. Partridge. "Even I don't know where it is."

Agata held out the brighter key but Turtle refused. "I'll take the original. That one your dad made. It's special."

Agata handed it over. Turtle held it in his hand, the metal cold and heavy, ticking gently. Something was happening inside although the surface was featureless and placid. Holes punched in the case showed sets of enmeshed gears clicking through each other.

"It's running," said Turtle.

It is, but it is very low on power.

He tried to grasp what they had seen: a station made just for Agata, a group of men who would kill to get the keys. These keys were amazingly powerful. But how did they work?

When the Mytro was born, she was formless, said 411. *She was the first, the first song. The Mytro sang these tracks, these stations into existence. Those keys you hold allow you to control this manifestation of her, the trains, the tracks, the stations. Those were the only ways you could understand her, so you gave it that form on this planet. Elsewhere, it is different.*

It will be very difficult to grasp what you hold in your hands, but I'm sure we will find a way to explain it. Remember, it is the thing that gives you control of the song … for a time.

"Can we just make a station where my parents are? Grab them? Get them away?" asked Agata.

Were it that easy. We are going to Italy. Your mother is there.

"Well," said Mr. Partridge. "I am fond of pizza."

A moment later, the train slowed and pulled into a stone station.

The sign above the rough-hewn door read *Maduria Spiaggia, Cimitero*.

"*Cimitero*," mused Mr. Partridge. "That's 'cemetery.' Delightful."

CHAPTER THIRTY-THREE

The Blue City

I will meet you back here, said the Nayzun. *I cannot leave the station.*

The Nayzun disembarked behind them, his footfalls silent on the rock floor. The walls were smooth sandstone and the only decoration was a tile inlay depicting a map of Italy with a golden dot at the heel of the boot-shaped peninsula. Three gas lamps shed little light on the rough rock walls and over the stone floor. The Nayzun stood before them, its long arm and fingers pointing toward the door.

"Before we go, can you tell us what Mr. Goode is trying to do with the Breach?" Turtle asked.

Slavery, said the Nayzun. *You will see, outside.*

"What do you mean 'slavery'?" asked Agata.

The Nayzun seemed to draw back to its full height.

For centuries, men have subverted your laws to use the Mytro for evil things. There already was violence on the Mytro, and the Mytro will not allow it. It has given you a reprieve to try to sort this out yourselves. You are important to what is happening these days, and the Mytro thinks you are capable. But humans have free will and the Mytro has misjudged them before. You have two of your hours to gather your family back together and stop this menace before the Breach manifests itself and the Mytro sets the rails on fire.

Agata sputtered. "Fire? What fire?"

When the Mytro is angry, it creates fire. Whoever is riding the rails or is in a station will die. Sometimes whole cities are destroyed. Your mother is near a station in this place. You must find her and get her out. If you do not, there's no telling what will happen.

"Can you stop it?" asked Turtle.

There is no need. If the Mytro catches fire, the men we are concerned with will be gone forever. You've been given a gift of time by the Mytro. Do not squander it.

"What are we trying to do? Who do we need to save?" asked Turtle.

You will see when you enter the camp. The rails say your mother is here, but she may be moved at any moment. Hurry.

Mr. Partridge opened the wooden door carefully and peeked out. A crisp, chilly wind began to pick up. Somewhere gulls cawed overhead. Mr. Partridge held the door for Turtle and Agata and followed them out.

Agata took Turtle's hand and the three walked into a bracing spray of cold, wet air. The door had opened onto a wide plain near a long, thin gray beach. The narrow, scudding clouds behind them were low on the water, and a faint mist told them it had just rained or was about to. The air was tinged with the smell of the sea. Agata shivered in Turtle's light jacket. The Nayzun ushered them out.

It was dark. They had travelled a few hours past sunset and the time zone here was six hours ahead of New York. In a few minutes, Turtle had moved thousands of miles, and he wondered if he would ever feel jet lag on these trips.

The first thing they saw on the outside was a massive field of blue plastic tents protected by a fence of thin slats connected together with wire. A riot of plastic bags and trash popped and thrashed in the wind and trash piled up at the corners of the fence, swirling up in little eddies in the wind.

The tents spread out from the edge of the field in impossibly long rows. There must have been miles of them, thought Turtle. There was the sound of children playing and people calling through the jungle of blue plastic. A little smoke rose up over some of them. Long lines of hanging clothes were strung from one tent pole to the next, and men and women moved from one tent to the other, calling in a singsong language Turtle didn't recognize. As he watched, it became clear—even from far away—that this was a tent city full of people.

"This is a group of North Africans who fled their homeland," said Mr. Partridge. "Terrible business. They're seeking asylum, but Italy won't take them and neither will their home countries."

Turtle had seen these sorts of things on the news but never in real life. It was as if an entire city had been transplanted here on this windswept field, the ocean pounding on one side and endless grass on the other.

The door they had opened was actually built into the grass of a low hill. It was hidden under an outcropping of soft sandstone and, although the inside was banded wood, the outside was made of the same stone as the hill. When closed, it would disappear from view completely. Turtle hoped they would be able to find it again. Then he spotted a small 13 etched into the stone, near the bottom. The Mytratti were clearly very thorough.

As they stood looking at the expanse of blue, a cry rose up over the city—a roar of a crowd, cheers and whistles filling the air. Turtle and Agata looked at each other and Mr. Partridge shrugged.

"Could be a football game," he said.

Their sneakers shot up puffs of dust as they walked toward the city. There were trails upon trails in the grass, and a few white Toyota trucks idled by a main road barred with a gate and checkpoint. The trash and the blue tents flapped in the ocean breeze. The evening dark was nearly complete, the only light coming from winking lights that twinkled between the blue plastic shelters. Over the water, the stars were coming out.

Turtle scanned the fence around the blue city. Agata's mother was somewhere in there.

As they approached the fence, they saw a wooden structure high above the tents, about a hundred meters away. It was cobbled together with pallets and painted bright red. In blaze yellow, slathered on the side like an accident, was the number 13.

"I think that's where we're going," said Agata. Turtle nodded.

They started moving along the edge of the city, away from the front gate. The fence was solid with only a few slats out of place. The main entrance, near the trucks, was apparently the only way in or out, although there were areas near the bottom where the fence had billowed out in the wind, leaving gaps where plastic bags collected and shredded in the breeze.

Finally they found an opening, the slats cracked at the base and the wire pushed out of the way. They tried to stay quiet, facing the back of a row of tents so close together there was barely any room between them. Mr. Partridge took up the rear. He was hunched over, trying to stay low, and doing a sort of pigeon walk that would have almost looked comical if they hadn't been so unsure of the danger.

Agata and Turtle scuttled through behind a tent and smelled something good and spicy cooking. They must have come in behind a mess hall or restaurant because they heard voices calling out orders and a clatter of dishes. Big cans of propane sat close to the tent, the gas tubes snaking under the plastic.

As they moved farther into the tent city, it was getting darker and the aisles were lit by weak LED lamps. Each tent had its own lamp, and there was a TV farther down the aisle they were walking, powered by an unseen gas generator. Families—mothers, fathers, children—were huddled around it, and no one noticed them going through except a few bored kids in ragged sweaters.

Turtle had no idea if they would get in trouble being here or not. The trucks out front seemed to be on guard patrol, but the fact that they snuck in under a hole in the fence suggested no one policed the perimeter much. Whatever was going on here was a bit less well-guarded than he originally imagined.

"So we head toward the wooden tower. It's not very far from here. I guess we just keep quiet and hope no one notices us," said Agata.

As they moved closer to the television, they saw the families were all watching a soccer game. When one of the teams scored, a cheer would rise up from the crowd, echoed by other groups farther away.

"They're so squeezed in here, and it's so cold now. What do they do in the winter?" asked Turtle.

"As I recall, many of them try to escape. This is far from any town or village, so they're often caught on the road. It's a tragedy, really," said Mr. Partridge.

"But the Mytro stop is right over that hill," said Turtle. "Why not lead them to it and away from here?"

"And where would they go?" said Mr. Partridge. "It's quite

complex, all this."

"Let's stay low. We can't get caught," said Agata.

With that, they skulked between two tents and started moving slowly through the camp, avoiding open flaps and large crowds.

A few rows in, however, they heard a quick *hiss*. Turtle turned. Facing them from across one of the rows was a bright-eyed boy, his dark skin burnished gold by the faded glimmer of the overhead lamps.

"Are you in need of help?" he asked, smiling.

CHAPTER THIRTY-FOUR

Building 13

The boy waved them over from his tent, so they went to him. He held out his hand to shake theirs.

"Hello," said the boy. "Are you looking for someone? Are you Americans?" he asked.

He was a small, skinny boy, about their age. He wore an old taped-up parka over a long-sleeve shirt and jeans that were a bit big on him. He continued to smile.

"I am. She's Spanish," said Turtle.

"I am Ehioze," said the boy. "I'm from Nigeria."

"Pleased to meet you," said Agata. "Do you live here?"

"I do. Are you Red Cross?" asked the boy, looking up at Mr. Partridge.

"No, we're not. We're looking for my mother," said Agata. "She's over there."

"In the center, building 13? That is a bad place," said Ehioze. He turned around to where his mother lay sleeping on a cot in the dim light of the LED lamp. He closed the tent flap and led them around the side. One of the teams scored another goal, and there was a clatter of cheers through the camp.

"I think I can take you," said Ehioze.

"You said that was a bad place?" said Turtle.

"It is. When we came here in a boat, the Italians put us here. They said it was only going to be for a short time For many days there were some British coming and going from the building. They say they are Red Cross, but they aren't dressed like Red Cross. It's cold here, and sometimes they don't have coats, and we don't see them drive here."

Agata looked at Turtle and they both nodded. "That's where we need to go, Ehioze," she said.

"We need to be very quiet," said Turtle.

"OK. Not a problem. Quiet is my, how do you say, specialty," he said, smiling. "Is this your father?"

Mr. Partridge chuckled. "No, just a family friend. Is your father here?" he asked.

"No, he is dead," said Ehioze. "I am with my mother. She's sick."

A chill went down Turtle's back.

"Thank you, Ehioze, for your help," he said.

Ehioze knew how to move between the tents without being noticed and helped them stay out of sight. He peeked around corners, waited for the cheers to rise up again, and then led them all across a darkened space between two tents, cutting corners and staying away from well-lit portions of the camp.

"It is a football match today. Egypt versus Saudi Arabia. Everyone is watching and making bets," said Ehioze. "I don't like football as much. But lucky for you everyone else does."

"Ehioze, why are you here?" asked Turtle.

"There is war in my country. We tried to get away as fast as we can, but many of us didn't make it," said Ehioze. He was surprisingly nonchalant in the retelling. "My mother didn't want us to grow up in such a place anymore, and she could not stand to be in the place where my sister died, in our home. So she took us on a boat here. We had money in Nigeria. I watched American television. We paid the captain to take us. We crashed on the beach a few months ago. They maybe will let us get out so my mother can work, so we are learning English and Italian just in case."

"How will you get out of here?" asked Turtle.

"Maybe the government will let us stay. It's called asylum. But until then we are to stay here."

Turtle thought about what Mr. Goode had said. Whole armies moved behind the battle lines. Men and women smuggled into hidden places.

"How many people are here?" asked Turtle.

"They said ten thousand, but it's more every day," said Ehioze. He led them down a dark aisle and to what looked like a stand of little kiosks where men were selling candy and cigarettes and other items laid out on blankets. Most of the men were watching television behind their stalls and didn't notice the children. Another was idly looking into his cell phone, his face illuminated by the glow of the bright screen.

They were close to the central building now, and they saw it was made of wooden pallets nailed together. Ehioze pointed to the upper level. As they looked more carefully, they noticed that the pallets were built up around a steel and concrete frame, like part of a bunker. There were stairs that led up, and the empty windows were obscured by white blowing curtains. The building was three stories tall and painted a chipped red. A stream of smoke came from the lower floor while a crowd inside cheered and still more jostled to look through the door. Another goal and another roar ripped the night in two.

The man with the cell phone looked up and right at them. Turtle and Agata swiftly moved back into the shadows. Ehioze waved, and the man simply went back to his screen, ignoring the boy. Ehioze said something in a different language, and the man replied curtly.

"Egypt is doing very well, it seems," said Ehioze as they moved along the perimeter of the square. "No one is kicking us out yet. Usually this place is very guarded."

The building loomed above them. Floodlights picked out the top floors, and a diesel generator chugged along next to the wall, pumping out noxious smoke. A splotch of oil on the ground showed where the exhaust pipe was belching out onto the now-dead grass. The ground was packed dirt, a little bit wet but mostly solid. There was a pile of rotten fruit near the corner of the building, and a skinny dog, his fat tongue lolling out of his mouth, was nuzzling through it. He barked once when he saw them and then went back to the fruit.

"How do we get in there?" asked Agata.

"Stay down and I'll let you in. There is a wall broken on one side. Follow me," he said.

They skulked past the edge of the building and around a

corner. Ehioze peeked through a hole in the makeshift wall. The room was packed with men, all smoking and yelling, watching a small television on the opposite wall. All eyes were on the game. The children slipped through and up the stairs in a flash. No one noticed them.

The second room was dark and empty. A small table and three chairs sat in a corner, and there were three cots on the floor next to military-issue backpacks. "The guards are outside," said Ehioze. "I saw one. He is my friend's older brother. He is very mean."

"Ehioze, thank you so much for your help. I know it was dangerous," said Turtle.

"Not dangerous," said Ehioze. "I was bored anyway. If you need me, find me in sector 6, row 10. We are tent 61022. Are you sure you are fine here by yourselves?"

"I guess we'll find out," said Agata.

Another cheer from below and the floorboards creaked above. Someone was up there. Ehioze slipped out after saying good-bye again.

Mr. Partridge placed his foot on the first step, and it creaked ominously.

"You stay down here," said Turtle. "We'll yell if there's trouble."

Mr. Partridge slowly removed his foot from the step.

"Are you certain?"

"We'll be fine, Mr. Partridge," said Agata.

The children crept up the stairs to the half-open door at the top of the flight and crouched down.

Agata had to stop herself from gasping.

CHAPTER THIRTY-FIVE

Goal

Turtle and Agata saw Mr. Goode pacing the floor of the upper room in Building 13, which was as warm and richly appointed as a modern CEO's office. The walls were painted, granite tile had been installed on the floor, and a dark wooden desk stood near one wall. There was a large computer and a set of file cabinets near the desk. A thick, red curtain covered the only window. A tall object, shaped much like a door and covered by a canvas sheet, lay propped against the far wall, and another object like it, covered in blue plastic, lay against the wall near the window.

Mr. Kincaid, Mr. Goode, and Mr. Martin were standing near the window while Agata's uncle and mother sat in wooden chairs by a glowing space heater. The room had its own small generator, the exhaust vented through a hole in the wall. It was a strangely opulent room that was essentially built into a shack.

From their vantage point, Turtle and Agata could see three more figures slightly obscured by some heavy furniture. A flat-screen television showed the game, a car commercial flickering on after a few instant replays of a goalie sliding out to snag a ball. The room was lit from above by nicely mounted track lighting dimmed just so.

Mr. Goode pushed back the curtain on the sprawling refugee camp. It was quiet now. The soccer game was winding down.

He waved an arm over the scene, taking in the entire camp in one sweeping gesture. Agata's mother sat next to him, her wrists held tightly together with plastic cuffs; a blaze-orange parka lay draped around her shoulders. She shivered in the cold as Mr. Goode, dressed in a black wool coat and a felt watch cap, paced the floor.

Agata's uncle Ernesto stared daggers at Mr. Goode. Ernesto had a nasty black eye, dark against his olive skin.

"Give this up, Goode," said Ernesto in English. "There is nothing in the world that will let this happen—no money, no influence, no politics. You think you've stumbled upon a gold mine. Many men before you have tried and failed to harness the Mytro. You will fail. What you are trying to do is impossible. What will you do when you get them there? How can you keep them hidden?"

"That's the magic," said Mr. Goode. "We're not using the Mytro to transport anything it hasn't transported before. But now we're using the station as a factory where we can store all the machines, all the people. We'll drive the other manufacturers out of business, and they'll never know where our products are coming from. We'll start with clothing, then we'll move into electronics. We can build other Breaches. We make a million pieces here, a million pieces there. We'll flood each market, control it, and these people will have comfortable lives to boot."

"What makes you think you can make this work?" asked Agata's mother. "Other men tried."

"Other men didn't have our research, our science. We understand the Mytro more than those primitive Mytratti ever did, even more than your husband does. My organization will soon be the first in history to claim complete control of the Mytro. You, of all people, should be rejoicing in that. The Breach is just the beginning. We're using it because Perdurabo already built it."

"It's madness. These men and women aren't yours. They're not slaves," said Ernesto.

"Slavery has nothing to do with it. These men and women want to work, and we're giving them the opportunity. When they sign our contract, we'll whisk them to a factory that is state-of-the-art and safe, away from this turmoil. Their African leaders don't want them and the Italians don't want them—that much is clear. They are stuck between countries. We can place them in any factory around the world at a moment's notice. What has always been the dream of the capitalist? To have a ready and willing workforce at the chime of a bell. Strikes? Call in my army of workers. Is your native workforce too expensive? Hire my men and women. They don't need huge factories and dormitories. In fact, their workplace doesn't even take up space. This isn't slavery, Ernesto, this is freedom. When they are ready to leave, they can go. But they won't want to leave."

"These people don't understand what they're signing up for. You control their destinies by placing them on the Mytro. They'll never be able to go home," said Ernesto.

"They have no home. Look at them. They're wretched, weak, and powerless. I give them work and a place to live and food to eat. These Italians, what do they have to offer? Nothing but fear and uncertainty. This is the modern lost tribe, men and women without a country forced to exist in limbo. I'm giving them a country. My country. We have powerful benefactors who will give them a factory the size of a city to live in. They will be fed and clothed. They will be able to teach their children and maintain their culture. They will be far from this turmoil."

"Far from this turmoil? In the wilds of Brazil? Deep in the Amazon? On a mountaintop? Under Barcelona in something that's about to collapse? They will be in a Gulag, unable to escape, unable to live freely except when they die. You're stealing them, hiding them, and making them work. How is that freedom?" yelled Agata's mother.

"Men have looked at the sea and seen dark, endless fear. They longed to cross her, they longed to scale mountains, they longed to put on seven-league boots and tromp through jungles and fields. The Mytro lets them have that power, have that freedom. To travel without moving? It's one of man's dreams, one we're going to finally realize. We will control the Mytro."

"You control nothing," spat Ernesto. "I won't argue this with you further. My niece is lost and frightened. Let us go and take me to her. We have nothing you want."

"You have nothing, to be sure, but the children have everything," said Mr. Goode.

"And you'll never find them," snarled Agata's mother. Turtle pulled Agata away from the stairs and they scuttled backwards. A hand closed over Turtle's shoulder and someone flipped him around. Agata gasped.

"Who are you?" asked a tall man with a British accent. He wore a coat like Mr. Goode's and carried a pistol.

"Red Cross?" asked Agata, hopefully.

"Likely story, love. You two. Who are you spying on then? Watching the game?"

"Turtle, run," said Agata quietly, under her breath. He didn't hear her the first time, and so she repeated it, slightly louder.

"Run, Turtle!"

Turtle ran.

CHAPTER THIRTY-SIX

Tent Station

The tall man lost his grip on Turtle as he twisted away and ran down the stairs to where a group of guards stood. They called out after him, but he squeaked between them. He began to sprint at full speed, running through prime numbers in his head with each breath, just as he did in track practice. He outran them all.

He saw Mr. Partridge, legs outspread, his arms against the wall. One of the guards was searching him. "Go, Turtle," cried Mr. Partridge.

Ehioze's "address"—sector 6, row 10—was booming in his head. He looked up at the poles at the end of each row, counting down each one as he ran. He passed row 9 and then came upon row 10. He was at a wide-open crossroads.

By now, more and more refugees noticed Turtle's flight from the central building into the packed dirt rows and aisles of the tent city. Most ignored him—after all, they saw Italians come through regularly—but a few began to call after him. By the time he reached sector 6, he had caused quite a stir.

Ehioze was outside his tent when Turtle arrived, breathless.

"Is all OK?" he asked, ushering Turtle into his tent.

"I don't know. I need your help."

"Do you need directions again?"

Turtle dropped his backpack on the table and rummaged through it, looking for the Key. Maybe it held something that could help them. Maybe it could do something.

"Can you lead me out of this place?" asked Turtle.

"There are ways out, yes, but I can't be found outside. I could be deported. We are waiting for transit visas so we can continue on."

"So maybe we need to find a way out here."

Turtle looked at the key closely. Most of the protrusions were decorative, but one tiny knob clicked softly as he turned it. Doing so seemed to wake something up inside it, causing the key to hum gently.

He remembered the Nayzun said the key listened to song. But what kind of song? A Nayzun song? Human? The key wasn't a key—it was a music box playing a strange, soft tune. Didn't the Nayzun say that the Mytro sang things into existence?

Turtle sang along. Ehioze sang as well, smiling.

"That's an old Nigerian song," he said, marveling at the key.

Turtle was stumped. He stared at the key in his hand, humming along.

And, like a magician's trick, out of the shadow, assembling itself out of empty space, was the faint outline of a station.

The tracks appeared. Ehioze nearly fell backwards, his eyes wide.

The train came, ghostly in the LED light.

How all this fit into a tent five feet wide and ten feet long, Ehioze and Turtle couldn't tell. The tent had expanded or they had contracted. Only one train pulled up in front of them, and then only the middle section, the front and back of the car hidden by the walls of the tent, but somehow the entire station fit into the space. The front flap of the tent moved slightly in the wind, and the station flickered. The tent, for a moment, was back and the station gone. The flap stopped moving, and the Mytro reappeared.

"Is this magic?" asked Ehioze.

"No, it's something else. Thank you for all your help," said Turtle.

Turtle heard scuffling and shouts outside. Someone yelled.

"They're looking for us," said Ehioze. "That's one of the guards."

"Then come with me," said Turtle.

"Where are we going?" asked Ehioze.

"We're going to Barcelona. But we'll be back—unless you don't want to come back."

The train doors dinged open.

"We are leaving the camp?"

Turtle thought for a minute. The map. He didn't have a copy. He'd need to find one if he was going to do anything in the Mytro.

"Yes, for a little while. We have to get something and then find someone."

"Is he on this train?"

"I'm not sure he's even on this planet. We have to hunt for him."

The boy nodded gravely. They boarded the train, and the doors dinged again, closing on a cushion of air. The key in Turtle's hand stopped humming, dead as he held it.

Barcelona. Agata's house. The portable door. He whispered the address under his breath.

Turtle sang again but this time the train knew where to go. Their pursuers barged into the tent behind him, but all they found was an empty tent lit by an LED lamp. The faint smell of train oil hung in the gloom.

CHAPTER THIRTY-SEVEN

Vulpine

The upper door sprang open, and Agata stood there, one of Mr. Goode's guards holding her shoulder like a vise. Mr. Goode's smile when he saw her was vulpine.

"Agata!" cried her mother.

Agata ran to her mother while Mr. Martin and three other guards stood back, their hands on something beneath their coats. Agata wrapped her arms around her mother and squeezed, taking in her scent, her soft exhale.

"*Te quiero, mama,*" Agata whispered.

"I love you, too, Agata."

"And with that charming reunion, I ask that what is ours be returned to us," said Mr. Goode.

One of the guards led Mr. Partridge, also cuffed, into the room.

"We found him outside," the guard said.

"Good evening, friends," said Mr. Partridge. "You don't know me, Madam, but I am a keen admirer of your husband's work."

"Ah, Mr. Partridge," said Mr. Goode, "so good of you to join us."

"Well, anywhere the Mytratti are I try to be. You know, to even out the bad with the good."

"You've got your key, Goode," said Mr. Kincaid. "Give me the money and I'm leaving. I'm done with this."

In a flash, Mr. Kincaid produced a pair of scissors. With a few snips, the backpack was cut, its contents spilled on the granite floor—the map, a flashlight, some food, a spare shirt.

The Conductor's Key, bright gold flashing, fell out last, and Mr. Kincaid caught it in trembling hands.

"You have it, now let us go," said Agata. She turned to him. "You have what you need."

"I'll let you go. First, we need to ensure the authenticity of the product," said Mr. Goode. "You'll go free after we've completed what we came here to do. But first, we'll send you to a bit of a novelty on the Mytro lines. You'll quite enjoy it, Ernesto."

The tall men came forward to grab Agata, her mother, and Ernesto. They led them forward through a door on the far wall. She tripped as she moved through, and as she fell, she heard someone—probably Mr. Kincaid—mumble something in the distance.

"But where's the boy? He has the other key!"

He's safe, thought Agata.

She fell and everything went dark.

CHAPTER THIRTY-EIGHT

The Mytratti Map

The train let Turtle and Ehioze off at Agata's father's office. They stepped through the portable door, and the world tilted slightly as they stepped into the study, still ransacked. Turtle motioned for silence.

He listened.

The house seemed empty.

"We have to find someone. He controls the tracks. I don't know where he is now, but I want to grab a map first. Maybe it will show us where they took Agata."

Turtle rummaged through the piles of papers until he found the map he had used when he decoded Mr. Llorente's message. It was still there, a little worse for wear, but intact.

He looked at it closely.

There was the whole of Europe, stop after stop. Some of the names were too big to fit on the map and were coded with numbers. Turtle noticed they were all prime, and "411" was somewhere in Russia, near Moscow. Was that 411's station? Or did it just connect to a longer list of stations elsewhere? Turtle didn't know and didn't have time to find out. They'd be on their way to the station soon enough.

"Whose home is this?" asked Ehioze. "It is very messy."

"It's Agata's. They broke everything here looking for something. Something we have."

"That thing you had? That made the ghost train?"

"Yes. They're bad men," said Turtle.

"There are always bad men in the camps. The bad outnumber the good too many times," said Ehioze. "But the good always win." He looked at the map, his fingers moving from station to station until he came to their camp on the heel of Italy's boot.

"That's where we were, yes?"

"Yes," said Turtle. He ran his finger over to Barcelona and pointed at the center of the city. "Now we're here."

"But how?" asked Ehioze.

"I have no idea."

Turtle scanned the map. Moscow? Is that where he would go? 411? Could he just say "411" and he'd go there? He doubted it. 411 was a code, not a station name. It was too risky.

Then, on the corner of the map, Turtle noticed a hand-written notation

The Hangar.

Didn't the Nayzun say that's where he was going? But why a Hangar? Where was it?

As they went over the map, they heard a train roll into the portable station. The door was ajar, and they heard someone move off the train, heavy shoes clomping on the stone floor.

Turtle looked around in a panic.

"Lads, lads, don't be afraid," said Mr. Adams, one of Mr. Goode's henchmen, from inside the station. "A chat, that's all."

Turtle slammed the door and wedged a broken wooden chair under the handle. Then Turtle closed the hasp and put an open padlock into the hole. The men on the other side pushed and pushed but couldn't get through.

Gunshots—three of them in quick succession. Then Mr. Adams began to try the door. He couldn't get it open. The chair held.

"We need to move this door. We have to get it out of here."

"Is it heavy?" asked Ehioze.

"I guess we'll find out."

It was, they found, very heavy.

CHAPTER THIRTY-NINE

Oubliette Italiano

Agata landed on her knees as she fell through the door. She craned her neck back and looked around to see the name of the station. Mr. Goode turned her head back.

"Where are we going?" asked Agata.

"We're not actually taking you anywhere, Agata, dear. We're leaving you in what I suspect is one of the most unique stations on the Mytro. Drag Mr. Partridge along, if you would, gentlemen. You see, there are no trains here," said Mr. Goode. "They don't stop on a schedule. There is only one way in, and no way out."

"Mother? Mama?" called Agata.

"We're here, Agata," called her mother.

"I'm here, too," said Ernesto.

"This is a very special portable station," said Mr. Goode. "It opens only one way and shuts immediately upon use. It's a terrible thing, really. A trap, of sorts, made by the Mytratti almost a century ago. I'm the only one who can save you. You'll stay here until I have what I want: both keys and both winders."

Agata blinked in the dimness. Three guttering gas lamps cast a weak light. The sign above the door read *Oubliette Italiano*. An oubliette, Agata remembered from history class, was a hole, a place you put people to forget about them.

"Give me the other key and you don't have to stay here. You're free," said Mr. Goode.

"I told you we don't have it," said Agata, struggling against the zip ties. "We didn't find it."

"I'm sure that's not true," he said.

Mr. Goode's men dumped Mr. Partridge on the floor, and he groaned softly. The station stank of dampness and cold; it seemed to be something like a cave—natural, dark, and vacant for centuries. An empty track bed was a few feet away, the ends stopped up with boulders carefully cemented into place.

As soon as Mr. Goode shut the door behind them, Agata rushed to try to open it. It was locked.

"Don't worry, Agata," said her mother. "Don't worry."

She was glad she finally could hug her mother, although the zip ties kept them from reaching out to each other. Her mother's warmth and smell calmed her. Ernesto kneeled down to tend to Mr. Partridge the best he could. Slowly, the teacher began waking up.

"I had both keys," said Agata. "My friend Turtle has the other one. It's safe."

"That's good," said Ernesto. "I'm glad you weren't hurt. Who's Turtle?"

"A friend I met in New York. He's been helping me. He'll find us and get us out of here."

"I hope so," said Agata's mother.

Mr. Partridge sat up.

"Right," he said. "Anyone have a knife?"

"There's a house key in my pocket, Niles," said Ernesto. "Good to see you."

"Good to see you, too, Ernesto. It's been too long. Your uncle and I were in university together, for a time," Mr. Partridge told Agata. "Now, let's get down to it then, and while I cut, you can fill your mother and uncle in on what you've seen today. Did you know she's met a Nayzun?"

Ernesto smiled.

"I knew she would," said Agata's uncle, his grin brightening the mood in the dark oubliette the way a campfire brightens a cold forest.

CHAPTER FORTY

Moonlight in the Alley

With a satisfying rip, Turtle and Ehioze finished wrapping the door in packing tape. They went around it multiple times, taking special care to wrap up the center.

"They'll never get out now," said Turtle.

Ehioze touched the door.

"An entire room, inside there?"

"An entire subway. Let's get this thing out of here."

It took them 15 minutes to lug the door down the winding staircase from the study.

"What is going on?" asked Ehioze, winded. "What is this door?"

Turtle tried to explain as quickly as he could, and Ehioze listened intently. He sat in Agata's living room, his eyes wide and a smile on his lips.

"This is amazing stuff," he said. "Sounds like science fiction."

"It kind of is," said Turtle. "So we have to take this door somewhere safe. I need your help carrying it. Then we're going to find Agata and get them all out."

"That is not a problem," said Ehioze. "I'm happy to help."

"You're not scared by all of this?" asked Turtle.

"Not particularly," said Ehioze. "Anything is better than watching football in the camp with my uncles."

Before they left, Turtle grabbed two packages of cookies from the kitchen and gave Ehioze a drink of water. They were both hungry, but there was little time to eat. They carried the door down to the street.

The Barcelona night was cool and calm. The little side street was empty, and although a few TVs flickered in the windows above, there was no movement. Turtle and Ehioze lugged the door toward La Rambla as Turtle related more of their adventures from the day as they walked.

"This Mytro sounds like a miracle," said Ehioze. "For refugees, especially."

"They used it during wars, I think," said Turtle. "I suppose it would work as a way to get people out of bad situations."

"I'd use it to bring my mother to England. She doesn't want to live in the camp anymore. She's very sad."

"We can help you out, I think. I'll show you how to run the Mytro when we have a bit more time."

Turtle checked the map. There was a station at the restaurant they came through the first time, and a little farther away, there looked to be a station down a dead-end street. They couldn't go back to the restaurant, and it was probably locked up anyway. They'd have to find the other Mytro stop.

They looked like two ants lugging a leaf through the streets, stopping often to put the door down and take a breath. There were a few people out on the street—some strolling home from warm-looking restaurants, others walking hurriedly down the dark street. One woman stopped talking on her cellphone abruptly as she watched the pair lug the door down the road.

Turtle wished he had a phone with GPS, but they used the detailed map to follow La Rambla past the shuttered newsstands and flower shops and up to a gated alleyway.

"Looks like we have to get through that," said Turtle, trying the lock. The wrought-iron gate was high and spiked with sharp metal spines. An iron 13 was worked into one corner and surrounded by iron flowers.

They slid the door and doorframe through the bars of the gate easily, careful not to snag the door latch, and Ehioze squeezed his slender body through the bars. He tried the lock from the other side, and it opened easily. Turtle came through and shut the gate behind him.

They faced a long, blank alley. Windows on the second floor looked down on dark gray cobblestones, and at the end of the alley was a blank brick wall.

There was very little light, and a large trash can and some bags leaned up against the back wall. Turtle moved the rubbish out of the way, disturbing something small and black that scampered off into the moonlit street.

"Now what?" said Turtle.

"Is there a door?" asked Ehioze. "A station?"

"Maybe," said Turtle. They leaned the door against the wall, and Turtle began pushing the bricks with his hands and then his shoulder, careful not to step in the trash. The wall moved. He pushed harder. The bricks slid in, and the wind picked up and began to suck them in.

Ehioze and Turtle grabbed the wooden door and quickly slipped through the hole in the bricks. They were in a cave-like space that was a bit bigger than the one under the restaurant. Ehioze whooped.

"That was great!" he said, catching his breath.

The train pulled up a moment later.

"The first time is fun," said Turtle with a yawn. "Try doing it all day long."

They muscled the door onto the train, and then Turtle whispered, "Hangar."

The train dinged once and began to move.

CHAPTER FORTY-ONE

The Hangar

Ehioze marveled at the tunnel that rushed past them and then disappeared.

A minute passed, then two, as they traveled in the dark.

Hungur, thought Turtle again. *Hangar.*

Still they moved in the dark. Then the barest hint of light, like a cloudy sunrise, surrounded them. As if they were passing through a glowing fog, the train cut out of the dark and into the light.

The train shuddered to a stop in a wide-open space nearly as dark as the tunnel itself but still lit by the miasmic light. The train doors opened, and they got off, lugging the portable door down the two steps and onto a floor that felt like it was made of crushed rock but was still strangely solid.

A dull glow came from parts of the huge room, and Turtle realized the Nayzuns were glowing. Their bodies casting a dim ghostlight on the edges of the room. They were listening, decided Turtle, as they stopped and looked at him. Something called from the tunnel behind them. It was a howl, almost, like metal twisting and breaking, like the whole tunnel was caving in. The heads of the Nayzuns all turned to look.

A Nayzun moved toward them.

"411?" asked Turtle over the roar.

No, the Nayzun said. Its voice was higher, strangely strident. It almost hurt Turtle's ears.

Ehioze stood staring in shock.

Come, said the Nayzun. *Leave the artifact.*

"This?" asked Turtle, motioning toward the portable door with his head. The Nayzun seemed to nod almost imperceptibly. They settled the door into the grit on the floor, and it sank into the ground and righted itself.

The Nayzun led Turtle and Ehioze into darkness, into a huge room full of old trains. Somewhere in the distance a piece of wood cracked, and somewhere closer someone was raking something smooth. The ceiling was too far away to see, and there were no walls, for they, too, were too far away from them to apprise. They could see only a floor of gray cinders that let up no dust as their sneakers dented the surface. Shallow tracks, the kind streetcars ran on, crisscrossed the floor into the dark distance, and every minute or so a new train would roar by on a distant track, sometimes close, sometimes far away, howling in the dark, the headlamp like a lonely campfire on a wide plain.

Turtle shuddered. The Nayzuns were in the dark, but they never saw the stars.

Somewhere above them was movement, and when Turtle's eyes became accustomed to the gloom, he was able to make out a Nayzun hoisting a train. He was cranking it by hand, his platform suspended by chains that were connected somewhere high over head. His long arms turned the crank slowly, raising the old train inch by inch. Something fell on Turtle's face, and he lifted his hand to see what it was—sand.

That train was broken by you humans, said the Nayzun. He gestured for Turtle to come forward. *They shot through it with their guns.*

As they moved through the gloom, Turtle could pick out other Nayzuns working on other trains. A pair of them had driven a train car onto a round platform and were turning it to head down another track. Amazingly, for all the work going on around them, the Hangar was quiet. Only the passing trains and the occasional clink of metal on metal disturbed the silence.

"All this for something no one ever uses?" asked Turtle.

The Mytro is used every moment of every one of your days. Your kind has ignored it for centuries, but there are others who use it in ways you have not yet imagined. Your planet is only one of the many terminals.

The Nayzun gestured with his long arm to an empty spot on the ground. Two tracks merged there, crossing over each other. *Stand there.*

"Where is 411?"

He is elsewhere.

Ehioze and Turtle stood at the crossroads. They waited. There was clanging in the dark, and a light began approaching them from their left side ... then the right. Then from all sides. Trains were coming down all four tracks, aiming for them in the center. Turtle turned and grabbed Ehioze.

Stay there, said the Nayzun.

"But—"

Stay, clanged a loud voice that surrounded them. The lights bore down on them, closer and closer. The clanging grew enormous.

Then it stopped.

CHAPTER FORTY-TWO

Voice In The Fire

The voice roared. Light surrounded them, a light so bright it was almost opaque. They could see the Nayzuns scuttling around beyond the circle that surrounded them.

Boy, you come here in the girl's stead?

Turtle and Ehioze stood stock-still. The voice was coming from the light.

"Agata is captured. She's back in Italy. She couldn't come," said Turtle.

Your kind has angered me for too long. This is a final insult.

"Please, I didn't do anything. There are others who are hurting us. Who are you?"

Mytro. King of Roads. The Endless One. I connected the stars before your kind crawled out of the swamps.

"I'm sorry if you're offended, but Agata and her parents are kidnapped. The Breach—"

The Breach, as they call it, is the least of their concerns. You brought an evil artifact here. Why did you bring the door?

"I wanted to keep it safe. The men were using it to break into Agata's home, and I wanted to bring it to Agata, to help her escape."

You were foolish for bringing it here. And you have a Key from that fool Perdurabo.

"Please, we're trying to help our friends," said Turtle. Ehioze reached out at the light and tried to touch it. His hand went through and he pulled it back.

"Very warm," he said.

This is not your fight, boy, and you should not be here. I am finished with you and your mistakes. I should not have been so kind to you humans.

The light began to glow brighter, get redder. Turtle and Ehioze huddled close as it got hotter and hotter. Turtle began to sweat.

Turtle remembered what the Nayzun said: when angered, the Mytro could fill the tunnels with fire at a whim.

The cinders at their feet began to glow bright red then melt into a black pool that stuck to their shoes like tar. It was closing in, whatever this strange power was.

A moment later, through the flames, something was pushing the portable door into the crossroads. It was another Nayzun. 411. Turtle was sure of it.

Inside, children, said 411, opening the door. The wood was beginning to burn.

The tape they used to secure the door had already burned off, and Ehioze lifted the padlock out of the hasp, freeing the door. Turtle took hold of the handle and pulled. A thin vein of melting plastic tape scalded Turtle's hand, leaving a welt shaped like a question mark. A moment later, they were inside the cool station. The Nayzun followed them in, and the door slammed shut behind them.

Then, suddenly, the door was gone.

"What happened?" asked Ehioze.

"I think the Mytro almost killed us," said Turtle.

I'm afraid, children, that you are correct.

CHAPTER FORTY-THREE

To the Breach

The Nayzun boarded a train and sang something to the rails. The train gave a little shudder, something Turtle had never seen. 411 beckoned for the boys to follow.

"We have to get Agata," said Turtle. "We need to go back."

In a moment, Turtle. We must do something first. We must close the Breach.

"But I don't have the winder. I can't use my Key. Is that what we need?"

I have the winder.

The Nayzun held up a winder on a leather cord. It was shinier than Agata's, newer.

"But you're—"

I am a Nayzun. I know I cannot have this. The Mytro is already angry with us. We are slaves to it, but we have grown to love this planet. We've watched you for so long, all of your kind. You war and fight and waste, but there is a goodness in you that we remember from our earliest days.

"Where did you get the winder?"

From Mr. Llorente. He was working to free the Nayzuns. He has understood the real madness of the Mytro. He was trying to help us.

"Wow," said Ehioze. He stared at the Nayzun, a look of amazement on his face, as the train began to move.

"'Wow' is right," said Turtle, sitting down. "We can help you, 411. I can use the Key. I can set you free."

The Nayzun stared straight ahead, quietly shaking his head.

It is too late. The Mytro is angry. It's about to break the Breach. It will destroy Barcelona. If you want the humans there to survive, we must prevent that.

"Whatever the Mytro is, it's enslaved you. Just like Mr. Goode wanted to enslave those people."

We're not people anymore. Everything we are is the Mytro.

"That can never be true. You're … free."

We shall see. We shall see. It's time to go back, Turtle Fulton. It's time to close the Breach.

CHAPTER FORTY-FOUR

Out of the Dark

Mr. Goode was a logistician at heart, and he had set up a system for the population of his factories. The women would board the Mytro first, with their children. The men would follow a few hours later. If the Mytro could carry 100 people—crammed like sardines—per car, they could clear out the camp overnight.

If there was any insurrection or, more likely, activity from the Italian military, they would let the refugees out in Rio, where the hope was they would be swallowed up by the sprawling favelas where Brazil's poor lived.

Mr. Kincaid, alone in Building 13, was in charge of loading the refugees onto the Mytro through a portable door. There were two in Goode's headquarters—the one that led to the oubliette and the other that led to a station built by Perdurabo himself. The rest of the men had gone to prepare the Breach for the first workers.

Mr. Kincaid looked out the window on the blue tents flapping in the wind. His heart thudded with fear. He hadn't wanted to do this—any of this—but Mr. Goode had ways of convincing poor urban archeologists to join his cause, mostly for the money. He needed the money. He kept telling himself that.

Some of Goode's men were already going from tent to tent preparing the women to move. Kincaid had seen what the Breach was going to look like—it was just another tent city, but one from which no one could escape. These workers would be underground forever—a fact Mr. Goode never mentioned to the refugee elders with whom he negotiated.

He could imagine the headlines tomorrow: "Italian Refugee Camp Found Empty." The mission of the Mytratti was to stay secret, and this would cast a bright light on just how these men and women disappeared. Mr. Goode had arranged a ship to sink off the coast of Sardinia to point the authorities in the other direction. Mr. Goode had prepared everything.

Forever. That word kept rolling in his mind. Forever. These men and women would live underground forever.

And Ernesto? Agata? Claire? The beautiful Claire? And Agata's father, wherever he was? Mr. Goode wouldn't let them get away.

"Kincaid. Everything's ready?" said one of the hired men, his bulk filling the doorway. Behind him a group of women and children stood quietly waiting. The doorway to their doom stood against the other wall, and Kincaid heard a train roll into the station. But he pointed to the oubliette.

"Yes, I think it is. After you," he said. "That's the one, right there."

"You sure? Mr. Goode said it was the bigger one," the big man asked.

"I'm sure," said Mr. Kincaid. The big man grabbed the door handle to the oubliette and twisted it like he was wringing out a towel.

In a flash, Ernesto was out of the oubliette. The back of his hand connected square across the big man's face, and Mr. Partridge, in a blaze of limbs, took the big man's legs out from under him and tackled him, holding his thick arms against his body. Agata and Claire came out, blinking in the light.

The train behind the other door chimed and rolled away.

Mr. Kincaid's head fell to his chest. His face red, he fought tears. Ernesto turned to Mr. Kincaid, who raised his arm in halfhearted defense.

"I'm sorry," he said. "I'm so sorry. Goode promised me the world. I can't do that to these people, no matter what he gives me."

"Where are they?" asked Ernesto.

"The Breach. They're preparing the Breach."

"The Breach is about to collapse," said Agata. "The Nayzun said so."

Mr. Kincaid shut the door on the line of women waiting to leave the refugee camp. A clamor of protests rose up.

"You promised us freedom!" cried one woman.

"You don't want this kind," said Mr. Kincaid as he shut the door.

"Please, go," said Mr. Kincaid. "I'm sorry, Agata. I let greed make my decisions."

Agata grabbed a few zip ties from the big man's pockets. She zipped the hired man's hands together while he still lay prone on the floor, and then Mr. Kincaid held out his hands and she zipped him tight. He nodded toward the other door.

"Get out while there's still time. More are coming any minute."

"We're going to the Breach. We have to stop this," said Agata.

Ernesto opened the door as another train rolled into the station.

They boarded, and Ernesto said the name of the huge, empty station made by one of the most elusive Mytratti of all. Above the door, as they rolled away, Agata read the name of this portable station: *Bahnof Perdurabo*.

CHAPTER FORTY-FIVE

Earth Station

The Nayzun showed Turtle how to wind the key, and it came alive in his hand. The ticking sounded like some kind of metal bug trapped in a jar.

Press the button there, on the top.

Turtle pressed a gold button, and the train stopped in the dark, just as they had before when the Nayzun had stopped the train. The whine from the key rose in pitch. He pressed it again. The key began to whirr.

You can turn the button to change the destination of any train you see. The key can also be used to play the song that calls stations anywhere and to make them permanent. When we reach the Breach, you will have to decide what to do.

"What can I do?" asked Ehioze.

"I need you to go back," said Turtle.

"But I want to help you, friend," said Ehioze.

"It's too dangerous," said Turtle.

The train stopped.

"Please Ehioze, please go home. I'll come for you and your mother."

Ehioze opened his arms.

"My friend, I will help you. You shared something magical with me," he said, hugging Turtle. "I am in your debt." Turtle hugged him back. The train doors opened.

The doors chimed, and the train rolled away. Ehioze stood next to Turtle. The Nayzun nodded toward what Turtle imagined to be the biggest station he had ever seen.

It was a huge terminal, seemingly miles long. Lights powered by gas generators rained down on the cold stone floor. Rows and rows of small huts had been built of concrete, and farther on, there was a long, brightly lit row of work tables that stretched on into horizon. This was a huge factory and living quarters, thought Turtle. Farther away, a series of blue tents were waiting for occupants.

This is where you humans would be slaves, said the Nayzun. *Like us.*

"What do we do?" asked Turtle.

When the Mytratti built this station, it was supposed to be something very special, but their powers were too weak to complete it. You are special, though, Paul Fulton. You have a gift. You were not chosen this morning to find Agata and go on this adventure by coincidence. Finish the Breach. You don't have much time.

Ominous creaks came from the high ceiling of the Breach. A stone fell and smacked a light, popping the bulb and casting some of the huts into darkness.

"What do I do?"

Imagine the song and sing.

Turtle stood, quietly.

"Why me?"

Because there is no one else. Sing.

What would the song sound like, Turtle thought. What was a song of completeness? He imagined completeness. He imagined holding Agata's hand, the feeling of waking up in a warm home, the feeling of eating dinner with his grandmother. He remembered the feeling of Agata's hug. He remembered sorrow, the death of his parents, the loneliness and the completion of his little family. He remembered love. He sang, and Ehioze joined him.

The rails listened. The song was wordless, Turtle rolling into falsetto, trilling notes he could have never reached in choir class. It was as if he were in a trance, the voice coming through him, a song in him, not of him.

"Well, well, well," said Mr. Goode, coming out of a concrete bunker not far from the rails. "Looks like the boy is beating us at our own game."

Keep singing, the Nayzun said.

"Zip these two up," said Mr. Goode, approaching the two boys. "Who was your tall friend?"

Turtle turned, still singing, but the Nayzun was gone.

He took a breath to sing the last note of the song.

The Breach creaked again. In the far distance, something cracked. More rocks fell. The edges of the Breach fell into darkness.

"What are you doing?" asked Mr. Goode. Mr. Martin and Mr. Adams came up to flank them, guns drawn. "Stop that!"

Keep going. I am here. I am always with you, said 411 from somewhere out of sight.

Turtle sang, Ehioze joining him when he could.

The far end of the Breach crashed down, the workbenches shattering under a torrent of broken rock. Winks of light came through the back wall of the Breach. Something blue shone out from behind it.

In a final, breathless note, Turtle and Ehioze finished the song. Somewhere nearby, the Nayzun screamed in their heads like a rasp of shredding metal. The back wall of the Breach fell with a crash. What it revealed was space. Behind the wall was the universe entire.

CHAPTER FORTY-SIX

Dragon Clouds

This was the end of it. The last stop. The last station. The Conductor's Key burned hot in Turtle's hand, and he almost dropped it until Ehioze reached over, grabbed it, and put it back in Turtle's backpack. Mr. Goode's strong hands pinched their forearms as he led them into the light. Mr. Martin and Mr. Adams stared at the back wall where stars dotted a dark sky. A planet with a swirling atmosphere spun in the distance, illuminated by the sun that was clearly behind them.

The stars out there shone as brightly as diamonds, the constellations lost in a ribbon of blue and purple and dark, deep black. The moon was full, and Turtle could see it as if it were in the room with him, the tracery of the craters looking like rotten lace.

The destruction of the Breach walls had revealed the true majesty of this station. They were looking at the universe through some sort of crystal. White and gold ribs arced from the floor into the darkness above. Along the edge of ceiling above them were Greek letters traced in bright gold, each one a foot high.

Mr. Goode followed their gaze and reached out a hand, one bejeweled finger pointing to each letter in turn. "It's Greek. It's quite a jarring statement, especially for a man who has been dead for 2,300 years."

"It basically says: 'Nothing exists except atoms and empty space; everything else is opinion.' A quote by Democritus. He never saw this, but his worldview would have changed with it," said Mr. Goode.

"The men who built this station were the giants of their day. They knew that one day we would destroy the laws of time and space, thanks to the Mytro. It is my goal to carry on their legacy. I had only ever seen the plans for this station. I thank you, boys, for completing it for me. I would have done it in my own image, on my own terms, but this is just fine. Changes quite a bit of my plan, that's for sure. Stop gawking, lads, and get over here."

The two goons walked Ehioze and Turtle over to Mr. Goode. Slowly, a group of men, covered in cement dust, came out of the hovels nearest the train. They shouted something at Ehioze, who answered.

"Keep the kid quiet, would you?" said Mr. Goode as he reached out to grab Turtle's backpack. Turtle moved out of his grasp.

"This isn't yours," shouted Turtle. "None of this is yours. If you keep doing this, the Mytro will be gone forever."

"That may be the case, but we won't let it go without a fight," said Mr. Goode. "But until then, it belongs to the Mytratti. This system has been with us since our inception, children, and you do not understand its power. I'm going to use it."

The workers called from their huts. They were approaching. Twenty of them in all, their faces caked in cement, remnants of their toil from building the Breach. Now they approached, angrily waving shovels and trowels.

"You'll never get it," said Turtle. "Just let us go."

Mr. Martin fired his gun somewhere off Turtle's left shoulder. Turtle's heart leapt and kept leaping, burning in his chest like an overwrought motor.

A train rolled into the station and out popped Agata and Mr. Partridge, followed by Ernesto and Claire. Surprised, Mr. Martin let Ehioze go for a moment. The boy called something out in his own language, and the workers started towards Mr. Goode and his men, anger flashing in their eyes.

"Tell them to get back," said Mr. Goode, panicking. A look of fear crossed his face as he backed away from the boys and onto the train.

"They're angry you lied to them," said Ehioze. "You said they'd be paid. Now they're wondering just what happened. One of them was hurt by falling rock. They want to hurt you."

"Tell them they'll be paid!" yelled Mr. Goode.

"Look, Mr. Goode, this wasn't in the contract. I was with you most of the way, but this is a bit much," said Mr. Adams. He backed toward the train that Agata and the others had just left, and he and Mr. Martin quickly hopped aboard. The doors shut. Turtle pressed the button on the top of the key then twisted it. The train began to roll forward. Inside, Mr. Goode screamed, "London, England. London!"

"The Hangar," whispered Turtle, and the key buzzed like a bee. The train rolled away.

"Turtle!" cried Agata. She ran to him and hugged him for a long time. When she let go, he felt warm.

"We'll have to find them now," said Mr. Partridge. "Unless our friend sent them somewhere else?"

Turtle nodded. "The Nayzuns showed me how to use the key. They're headed for the Hangar. I just wonder what will happen when they get there."

"The key to science, I think, is experimentation," said Ernesto. He shook Turtle's hand. Claire hugged him.

"You guys did great. It sounds like it was a wild ride," said Claire.

"What about Mr. Kincaid?" asked Turtle.

"He's tied up. We'll deal with him later," said Mr. Partridge.

The key buzzed in his hand. He heard 411's voice in his head.

Her father is beyond this station, Paul. We must fetch him but we cannot now. The Mytro nearly destroyed itself as you were completing the Breach. But now you are in control. We will help you find him. I remember myself, now.

"Did you hear that?" asked Turtle.

"I did," said Agata, marveling.

You've given me freedom, children. My name was Carlos Llorente. I remember that now. I remember falling, I remember losing my brother, and I remember being lost until the Nayzuns found me. Over time, without feeling or knowing what was happening, the Mytro changed me. It has been so, so long. I pray that your father does not undergo the same transformation, in the dark, that I did. I believe we can stop it.

It will take time.

I can keep the Mytro in check for a moment. When you completed the station, you completed me. I will ride the rails for you to find what you seek.

"Thank you, *Abuelo*," whispered Agata. "For everything."

CHAPTER FORTY-SEVEN

The Door in the Wall

Turtle and Agata stood holding hands, their hair buffeted by the wind from the Mytro. They looked out on the Breach, the wide expanse of space, the impossibilities there. Her father was somewhere there, out in the dark, the barest hint of stars winking in the endless expanse of the Earth Station.

Agata's mother and Ernesto came up behind them and put a hand on each of their shoulders. "You did well. As well as you could," said Ernesto.

"But Papa," said Agata. Tears rose in her eyes, and Turtle resisted the urge to wipe them away.

"We'll find him," said Agata's mother. Turtle nodded. "We have to fix the damage Goode did and help the people he lied to."

"You heard Carlos," said Turtle. "Your father is out there, somewhere."

Agata nodded, tears stopping like she was pulling them back into a bottle. Her chin was set, her demeanor strong and brave. She squeezed Turtle's hand tightly as the wind died and the stars faded out.

411—Carlos—spoke again.

You must give us time, he said.

"Then we'll wait," said Agata.

By then, Agata and Turtle would be ready. Turtle would know the Mytro like the back of his hand. He would memorize the map and see Agata as often as he could.

Turtle reached around to pull his backpack to the front and take out the shining Conductor's Key.

"This is yours, Ernesto. This is the other key," he said.

Ernesto stopped him, placing a hand on his.

"It's yours, now. Agata has the other. You two were chosen, and you two must keep them. If something changes, we'll come to get it, but until then we've angered the Mytro enough for a day."

"What about Ehioze?" asked Turtle.

"We'll get everyone to safety. One of the things the Mytratti did was create ways for workers to live comfortably without giving up the secrets of the rails – and most of those secrets have to do with money," said Ernesto. "We'll get them and Ehioze's family to safety.

Turtle nodded solemnly. He tugged the backpack back around his body and settled the straps onto his shoulders. The maps there were heavy enough, but the golden key was heavier. It seemed to still radiate heat into his back through the nylon fabric, and he wondered if it was just his imagination or if it was still hot from the exertion they had put it through.

The train roared up a moment later, and they boarded. They each took seats, and as the wicker settled around them, the train rocketed out of the station and into the darkness.

"Home," said Turtle. Then Agata said it. Then Ernesto. Then Agata's mother. Home.

The wind was picking up again as they left the Breach. For a brief second, as they passed from the station into the dark, Turtle almost saw the Nayzun as a bolt of pure, white light. But it was just for a second and then it was gone.

CHAPTER FORTY-EIGHT

Paella

Moments later Ernesto was holding the door open for Turtle at the Bay Ridge Fifth Avenue Theatre station in Brooklyn.

"We'll see you soon, Turtle. We're going to need your help," he said. "Thank you. We couldn't have done this without you."

"What about Mr. Kincaid?"

"We'll go and get him when we're ready. Ernesto and I need to make plans," said Agata's mother.

"Please don't hurt him," said Turtle, thinking of Nick and Nate.

"We know," said Ernesto. "He was confused. It is the problem with the Mytro. It makes men blind to their foolishness. The Mytratti are massing again, but there is a group now that will oppose them."

Turtle nodded. The Mytro bells chimed above him, and the doors began to hiss shut. "Turtle!" said Agata. He reached out to put his hand on the door, the mechanism clunking somewhere near the top of the door, the hydraulics pushing gently against his hand.

"Thank you, Turtle," said Agata.

"I'll see you again," he said, certain he would. He had his own map, and Barcelona was only a moment away.

"Definitely," she said.

The Mytro doors hushed shut behind him, and he turned to watch Agata and her mother waving from their seats. Ernesto and Mr. Partridge smiled at him as they rode into the darkness. The train rattled away, disappearing as if it had never been here, taking them back to Barcelona.

Turtle walked to the exit door and pushed. It gave for a second and then opened, popping him out behind the old Alpine movie theatre. His sudden appearance startled a small black cat nosing through a bag of garbage. It was late and the full moon was bright against the sky, casting long shadows over the trash cans and wooden pallets stacked in the alley. The familiar smell of Brooklyn came back to him in a rush: someone cooking fish somewhere nearby, the exhaust, the tree buds popping in the night air. Under it all was the smell of the ocean, not far off. It reminded him a little of Barcelona and that delicious paella.

He looked at his watch. It was midnight. He had been gone for six hours, and in that time he had seen and done so much that he could hardly believe it. It was a strange feeling to have travelled so far yet spent so little time getting there. His grandmother would be upset, he was sure.

The moon rose like a gift over Brooklyn. He was home. He walked down the alley into the street and then up the sidewalk to home. He clutched the map in his pocket, the complete index, and began planning his route to school. He imagined the lines of the Mytro like veins of bright silver in the dark world, rivers of thought and space and time that would, soon enough, carry him wherever he wanted to go.

As he rounded the corner, his heart sank. Two patrol cars, their lights flashing, were parked outside. A police officer sat in one of them, talking on the radio. When Turtle approached the house, he rolled down the window.

"Paul Fulton?" he asked.

"Yes, sir," he replied.

"Your grandmother's been worried. Get inside, son."

His grandmother was sitting at the kitchen table with a police officer. She looked so small. Her white, curly hair framed her lined face, her smudged glasses, her blue eyes—his mother's eyes— blinking back at him. When Turtle walked in, she stood up and grabbed him, hugging him close. She was rarely stern with him, but this time her face hardened.

"You scared me, Paul. I don't like that," she said. "Where were you?"

The discussion was quick and painless. He explained that he

had fallen asleep on the train and ended up in Queens. Then with outages, reroutings, and the rest of it, he had ridden for hours trying to get back to Brooklyn. Finally, he said, he had walked from Park Slope, a good hour's hike.

"Where's your cell phone?" asked the officer.

His grandmother looked down at the table. "I didn't buy him one yet. I guess he's been my boy for so long, I never thought I could lose him," she said.

"I'm sorry, Grandma," said Turtle. His face felt hot, and he was near tears. He was most disappointed that he couldn't share what he discovered, that he couldn't bring her down to the alley and take her anywhere in the world.

Ten minutes later, the police left, advising him to keep his grandma apprised of his travels around town and that they didn't want to have to come back again for the same complaint.

"Buy that boy a cell phone, ma'am," said one of the officers before they drove away. His grandmother waved them good-bye.

"Paul, please, never again," she said, hugging him once more. It was good to be home with her. She was his family.

"Don't worry," said Turtle. "It's the first and last time."

In bed, Turtle thought about Agata. They had been around the world and back, yet there was no evidence of his leaving. It was impossible, he thought, but it had happened. The world had changed for him, but the space he took up in it was the same. He closed his eyes and dozed off.

When he woke, he couldn't tell if it was morning or night. A voice from the kitchen brought the topsy-turvy world back into focus, and he turned his head to look at the cable box next to the TV. It was 6:46—presumably in the morning—he had been asleep for hours.

His grandmother was downstairs in the kitchen, probably talking to one of her chef friends on the phone. He heard her laugh and the tinkle of dishes in the sink. The water ran for a moment and then she shut it off. He imagined her standing over the sink, cleaning the dishes he had used earlier (he regretted not cleaning up before leaving the house the previous afternoon) and talking to a pastry cook she knew from Naples.

As the will to sleep was sapped from him, he sat up in bed and placed both feet on the wooden parquet floor.

Everything was back where it should be.

For a moment, Turtle wondered if he actually just slept through the day, and as strange as it sounded, he could have been dreaming. Panic rose in his chest as he looked around the room for his backpack. It was hanging on the doorknob.

He thought of the Nayzuns and their ceaseless work. He thought of Mr. Kincaid's madness and anger and what he would have to tell Nick and Nate when he saw them at school.

He sat up. He had a way to find out if this was all real. Turtle unzipped the backpack and stuck in a hand. He rummaged around, his heart sinking, until his fingers closed around a cold metal rod. He instantly knew what it was. The Key. It was safe, and he was in charge of it. Next to it were the maps he would study until he heard from Agata again. Relieved, he squeezed the second Conductor's Key tight in his left hand and let it go.

"Paul? Are you up?" said his grandmother from the kitchen.

"Sure, Grandma," he called.

"You sure you don't want to sleep a bit more? It's Saturday."

"No, Grandma. I'm fine."

"Pancakes?"

"Yes, please, Grandma," he said and walked through the house and down into the kitchen. As he ate, he thought of Barcelona.

"Grandma, do you know how to make paella?" he asked.

"Sure. Why do you ask?"

"I had some with a friend. I really liked it. I'd like to have it again."

"Sure thing, kiddo. Sure thing," she said. "We'll cook it up today."

The sun rose over the city, bright and pure. He was home. He was complete.

ACKNOWLEDGEMENTS

Writing fiction is so far from my day-to-day experience that I needed a lot of help. Special thanks to my editing team, Chris Nesi and Sharon Honeycutt. Also thanks to Bryce Durbin for his excellent illustrations. Also thanks to the TechCrunch team for putting up with me.

Thanks to Kio Stark for her advice on self-publishing and Slava Rubin and his team at Indiegogo for their assistance in setting up my campaign. Thanks to Steve Long for shooting the intro and outro videos.

My inspirations have always been my father, Robert, and my teachers, Tony Earley and Theresa DeFrancis. My mother, Mirka, taught me to love travel.

Special Thanks to these very special contributors. I sincerely appreciate your donations.

Daniel O Connell
Edward Zitron
Cyan Banister
Bret Ioli
Thomas Kupracz
Jason Kneen
Kerem Ozkan
Matt Sandy
James Sung
Nicolas Saltarelli
Ahmed Salama

A very sincere thanks to Michael Arrington who has always bet on me.

Also thank you to my Mytratti, the secret masters of the Mytro, who went above and beyond the call of duty.

Ariel Adams	Mircea Goia	Thomas Newbold
Jordan Anderson	Paul Goudas	Marco Peluso
Alexandria Aranoff	Paula Gould	Piotr Peszko
Tamara Barr	Michael Green	Matthew Podboy
William Beckler	Todd Haselton	Joseph Puopolo
Ben Biron	Annie Heckenberger	Benita Raczka
Aaron Bond	Steven Hennig	Mayer Reich
Sam Boutros	Jim Herbeck	Andy Rosenbaum
Ahmed Bouzid	Mary Herbeck-Smith	Shy Rosenzweig
Charlie Brock	Leslie Hitchcock	Larry Salibra
Teresa Broering	Bassam Jalgha	Steve Sargent
Matt Burke	Scott Jangro	Bret Schlussman
Maximilian Busser	Bala Kamallakharan	Peggy Shaughnessy
Donal Cahalane	Willem Kamerman	Emilie Slaby
Chris Cannon	Chris Kiklas	Adam Sohmer
Christian Cantrell	Chad Koehler	Richard Svinkin
Steven Carter	Noah Kravitz	Deborah Szajngarten
Arnie Chaudhuri	Manu Kumar	Keith Teare
Alexandru Circei	Gregory Kumparak	Karen Thomas
Jeff Clavier	Richard Lai	Kim Titus
Joshua Cline	Seth Levy	Elliot Tomaeno
Jack Conte	Carm Lyman	Alexandra Tsotsis
Kelly Crummey	Jarek Markocki	Alexander Tsoukias
Jude Divierte	Scott McKenzie	John Van Den
Betsy Durbin	Bob Michiels	Nieuwenhuizen
Amy Ferguson	Ken Minn	Brian Wall
Martha Fischer	Lynne Mulholland	Peter Weber
Marc Flores	John Murillo	Hussein Yahfoufi
Lior Gavra	Eugene Murphy	Stacie Yu

This book is for Kasper.
The next one will be for Milla.
The final one will be for Guthrie.
All of these books, all my best work, and my heart belong to Joanna.